THIS life

The Companion Guide Tom McGregor

Tom McGregor is the pseudonym of a well-known novelist and journalist. The author of 18 books, he lives and works in London.

THIS life

The Companion Guide Tom McGregor

PENGUIN BOOKS BBC BOOKS

PENGUIN BOOKS
BBC BOOKS

Published by the Penguin Group and BBC Worldwide Ltd
Penguin Books Ltd, 27 Wrights Lane, London W8 5TZ, England
Penguin Putnam Inc., 375 Hudson Street, New York, New York 10014, USA
Penguin Books Australia Ltd, Ringwood, Victoria, Australia
Penguin Books Canada Ltd, 10 Alcorn Avenue, Toronto, Ontario, Canada M4V 3B2
Penguin Books (NZ) Ltd, 182–190 Wairau Road, Auckland 10, New Zealand

Penguin Books Ltd, Registered Offices: Harmondsworth, Middlesex, England

First published 1997
1 3 5 7 9 10 8 6 4 2

ISBN 0-14-027432-4

Based on the television series produced by World Productions Limited for the BBC

Text copyright © Tom McGregor, 1997
All rights reserved

The moral right of the author has been asserted

Design and artwork by The Bridgewater Book Company
Art Director: Stephen Parker
Photographs © BBC, 1996 and 1997
Photography by: Joss Barratt, Nicky Johnston, Mark Lawrence, David Venni

Set in Meta and Letter Gothic
Printed and bound in England by Butler and Tanner Ltd, Frome and London

BBC ™ used under licence

THIS Life Contents

Introduction

At last – the indispensable guide to the cult series of the 90s.

This companion volume contains everything you ever wanted to know (and some things you never wanted to know) about the realities of *This Life* and the characters who lead it. Taking you behind the scenes, to chambers and bedchambers, to marriage and Miles, alcohol and Anna, to moaning and Milly and much more, it provides the definitive guide to safe sex, dangerous sex, courting, house-sharing, plumbing, drinking, soliciting, dating, fighting, eating, briefing and debriefing – as lived to the ground-breaking full in *This Life*.

Featuring interviews with the cast and crew, memorable lines from the series, a challenging quiz and statistics from the downright silly to the desperately serious, this fully illustrated volume is the ultimate companion for anyone who shares *This Life*.

THIS Life The Accused

ANNA (Daniela Nardini): A JUNIOR BARRISTER
'I believe in booze. It's a great leveller'

MILES (Jack Davenport): DITTO
'A Greek tragedy waiting to happen'

MILLY (Amitra Dhiri): A SOLICITOR
'Am I boring?'

WARREN (Jason Hughes):
A SOON TO BE EX-SOLICITOR
'Haven't you heard? I'm at odds with Mother Nature'

EGG (Andrew Lincoln): DITTO
'When I'm a world class chef I'm going to change my name to Benedict'

JERRY (Paul Copley): EGG'S DAD
'This isn't drugs. This is me. I'm amazing!'

FERDY (Ramon Tikaram): A COURIER
'I'm not gay'

KELLY (Sacha Craise): A RECEPTIONIST
'Are you calling me fat?'

RACHEL (Natasha Little): A TRAINEE SOLICITOR
'Outgoing single female who's out a lot and loves to clean'

LENNY (Tony Curran): A PLUMBER
'There's a Glaswegian in our boiler'

HOOPERMAN (Geoffrey Bateman):
HEAD OF CHAMBERS
'I really must ring for a sushi delivery'

FRANCESCA (Rachel Fielding): MILES'S FIANCÉE
'Suddenly I'm this screaming harpy after his sperm'

O'DONNELL (David Mallinson): MILLY'S BOSS
'My emphasis may have been misleading'

DELILAH (Charlotte Bicknell): A BULIMIC MODEL
'Can I borrow some money?'

MONTGOMERY (Michael Elwin): MILES'S FATHER
'You're actually a totally corrupt, self-serving bastard'

JO (Steve John Shepherd): A BARRISTER'S CLERK
'I'll be looking suave, sophisticated...'

KIRA (Luisa Bradshaw-White):
A BUDDING RECEPTIONIST
'Who says romance is dead?'

NICKY (Juliet Cowan): A COOK
'As I said, it's not exactly jumping out there'

GRAHAM (Cyril Nri): A BARRISTER
'Dark horse, aren't you?'

SARAH (Clare Clifford): A SOLICITOR
'Be direct. I like that...'

THE THERAPIST (Gillian McCutcheon)
'   '

THIS Lifestyle

Lifestyle manuals are all the rage – and none more so than the essential guide to *This Life*, the bible for those who want to tread the route to inner harmony; the companion for those who seek emotional enrichment, vibrant health and lasting happiness as exemplified by our friends in the house. How exactly did they do it?

There are two schools of thought. One is that in their quest for enlightenment they looked at their inner needs and, after quiet contemplation, arrived at what psychologists call the 'fifth level of motivation' – a realisation of their self-actualisation needs. Not many people know what this means and there are few pupils at this school.

The other training establishment espouses the theory that 'a lot of what you like does you good'.

The good news is that both schools are founded on the same basic principles:

A Balanced Diet

This is important. Nourishment is all. Miles still has some way to go ('breakfast is for wimps') but the others know you have to seize the day with something sustaining. Milly breakfasts on melon, Warren on yogurt and Egg on toast. Anna's morning victuals – a fag, a coffee and a vitamin pill – demonstrate an impressively minimalist approach, although she does occasionally experiment with alternatives. She has twice been known to demolish a fry-up, has been spotted munching a slice of bread and, on one particularly fraught occasion, downed a glass of Soave. Variety, says Anna, is the key.

Lunch can be a tricky occasion for city slickers. Time is of the essence, but Kira always finds the time to devour a healthy plateful of spag boll at the local caff. Kelly, poor thing, is stuck in reception but seeks solace in light snacks comprising turkey thighs, chocolate and crisps. The others either grab a sandwich (why is 'grab' the only verb you're allowed to use with a sandwich?) or eat out. See THIS LIFE'S GUIDE TO EATING OUT.

Just as the Famous Five accompanied every meal with lashings of ginger pop, their infamous elders opt for lashings of alcohol. Beer from the bottle is *de rigeur* as an aperitif. White wines – Soave and Chardonnay in particular – are in the ascendant with the girls whilst the boys veer towards the more macho red. Red is also Milly's preferred tipple when she's taking one of her historic baths.

Wine is generally accompanied by food. Anna has a penchant for frozen pasta and pot noodle, whereas Miles is partial to a tin of curry. House meals tend to be rather grander affairs, featuring fresh pasta with imaginative ingredients, coq au vin and, after Ferdy moves in, a lot of hot stuff.

Food Combining

There is a conflict of opinion as to exactly what this means. Milly says it means not mixing proteins and carbohydrates. Ferdy reckons it involves blending dope into your cake mix. Delilah reckons that you can combine anything with everything but with disastrous results. Anna swears it means it's illegal to eat food without alcohol. Egg says it's just a fancy word for a recipe. Warren is in confusion about it and hopes a session of therapy will lead to the answer.

ANNA HAS THE FINAL WORD ON FOOD COMBINING:

'I'd like a Veneziana with a relationship on the side.'

Drugs

JERRY: **'I hope he didn't rip us off.'**
ANNA: **'Of course he ripped us off. Getting ripped off is what it's all about.'**

This Lifers have a drug problem – drugs are illegal so you can't actually recommend them as food supplements. And while most of our friends in the house reckon that dope should be legalised, they do concede that if all drugs were made legal then their work would suffer: many is the time they've had to defend or prosecute users and dealers. Anna even found herself in the unhappy position of having to defend her own dealer. Strictly speaking, she should have refused to take the case on grounds of 'embarrassment' (mortification, more like), but she would have had to explain the whole situation. 'I know this man and I know he's guilty – he's my dealer' is not a career-boosting statement.

    Anna swore to give up drugs after that. We didn't believe her. We were right.

Dope

The drug for all reasons. Egg's the biggest dope fiend and rare is the day that passes without a spliff. He was even spotted smoking a joint with his cancer-victim client at a pavement café. Then he went back to work and wittered to Warren. Not recommended as a career move.

    Most memorable Dope Smoking Moment: Miles and Egg off their heads when the police came looking for Ferdy. Egg got the giggles and

WARREN GOES ON A HEALTH KICK:

'Right. That's it. I'm off the booze. For ever. I mean it. It's drugs only from now on.'

Miles Got Very Angry with Ferdy for 'Compromising three people's jobs to cover his own arse'. The scene led to *This Life*'s most expensive loo-flush: £80 of dope went down the pan.

Dope also features in cooking. Anna was slow off the mark on this one, telling Ferdy that God invented Sainsbury's so that you don't have to make biscuits any more. But Ferdy's biscuits had an ingredient you won't find at any supermarket...

Ecstasy

Popular at raves. Anna knows the dangers, though: 'Either you drop down dead or you have the night of your life. The latter is statistically more likely.' Ferdy and Lenny certainly had the night of their lives at the wedding: in ecstasy on Ecstasy and breaking wedding etiquette in the loo.

Coke

Expensive (you need a tenner to shove up your nose). Not recommended either. It very nearly led to the Fall of Anna when Graham caught her snorting the stuff in the chambers' loo.

Speed

Also known as whizz. Plays a small cameo role in *This Life* and was spotted at Miles's stag night.

Smack

Do you want to end up like Delilah and Truelove? A real no-no in *This Life*. Led Miles to the HIV clinic.

PS: All the above drugs are illegal and it is a criminal offence to consume or possess them. Consult a barrister or a solicitor for further information.

ANNA SMOKING A SPLIFF:

'Last time I had stuff this good I had a dream about Michael Portillo. It was good, actually.'

A Healthy Mind

The brain needs food as well as the body – so don't neglect those little grey cells. Here is some challenging reading material as recommended in _This Life_:

KNAVE, FIESTA, RAZZLE AND HUSTLER

Illustrated titles with a strong anatomical and biological bias. Handy formats make them easy to slip under the mattress. Some of these titles are interactive, with sections entitled 'Readers' Wives'. A five-star recommendation from Miles.

MAKING LOVE THAT LASTS

Shortlisted by Milly, but later withdrawn on the grounds of being a contradiction in terms. Replaced by O'Donnell's briefs.

THE TAKING OF PRINCESS SELINA

A learned and erudite study of the reciprocity of arousal, the versatility of wooden objects and the exploration of unlikely orifices. An under-appreciated present from Egg to Milly.

NEW MUSICAL EXPRESS, MATCH AND FOOTBALL MONTHLY

Part of Egg's 'How to Write a Blockbuster' canon.

DEADLY WISHES

Egg's blockbuster. Its wish came true and it died shortly after conception.

ANNA KARENINA

Anna's favourite book. A parallel element here? Anna K threw herself onto the rails – our Anna is about to veer right off them. A very good read and best accompanied by a bottle of Soave and some frozen pasta. Keep cigarettes handy at all times.

KELLY'S HOLIDAY DIET GOES HELLISHLY WRONG:

KIRA:

'Do you want to go away or not?'

KELLY:

'Not if it means I can't eat for three months. I really have got big bones! I could stitch my mouth up for a year and I wouldn't get any smaller!'

KIRA:

'You'd talk less shite, though.'

THIS Life's Guide
To Eating Out

This Lifers have an aptitude for Eating Out. Where there is food, after all, there is alcohol. Anna and Miles are the most proficient exponents of the art, although the latter has yet to learn that one is supposed to remain seated throughout. He has an alarming propensity for picking an argument, disturbing the entire restaurant and then bolting from the table. In his defence, Miles claims that his father's presence at the same table is usually the cause of this behaviour. We're not convinced and suspect a Bill-Paying Allergy. After all, when he eats at Egg's café, he never coughs up. Maybe that's what attracted him to Delilah: she dispensed with food altogether and was happy dining off the cheaper alternative of wine and cigarettes.

Anna also displays curious tendencies when Eating Out. One is to wear a belt instead of a skirt and to display her legs to all and sundry. Another is to kiss lesbians at table – something every good girl is warned against at an early age. Still, Anna never claimed to be good: 'I'm bad fairy,' she once said.

Egg and Milly issue repeated threats to go out to dinner together, but the meal never materialises. Milly does eventually eat out – with O'Donnell. It's the first of several meals, some in the office, others in restaurants and one particularly memorable one in O'Donnell's flat.

Things To Do With An Egg

Make Egg Nog — **a drink of eggs and hot beer or spirits.
(Sounds revolting. Better to make Egg snog.)**

Grow Egg Plants

Buy an Egg Whisk
and Beat Raw Eggs **Milly already has one.**

Be a Good Egg!

Put all Your Eggs into One Basket

Take Eggs for Money

Teach Your Grandmother to Suck Eggs

Tread Upon Eggs

Egg Someone On!

Egg's
Recipe For Disaster

Take £80 of housekeeping money and blow £73.80 on gambling. Buy a lot of spinach and loads of garlic with the change. Inform your housemates you were mugged and hope for the best. You will generally find that the worst happens. Anna will threaten to sever your manhood with a cheese grater and Warren will moan that all he's got left to his name is 'an individual fruit pie' (but then we knew that already).

Anna's Guide
To Abstinence

- **JUST SAY 'NO!'** to prescription drugs.
- **DO NOT DRINK WATER** – it's contaminated.
- **GET TRENDY** – get Downshifting.
Shift down from Marlboro to Silk Cut.
The benefits are immediate.
- **SET A NEW TREND –** get Upshifting.
Shift up from one bottle to two.
- **LET SARAH PAY FOR DINNER –** but don't go to
bed with her. Remember – abstinence makes
the heart grow fonder.
- **GO TO A RAVE** instead of going to bed
(saves on sleep).

Anna's Guide To Alcohol

Wine

Anna has a refreshingly unfussy attitude to wine. Not for her the agonies of what to drink when and with what food: she discovered long ago that Soave Goes With Everything.

For a girl who's not afraid to experiment in other areas of her life (see KISSING LESBIANS) Anna's pretty rigid about sticking to Soave. While she's happy to drink practically everything else, she only ever buys the Italian stuff. It's in her blood – literally. And although Anna's purchasing power is limited in other directions, she seems to have an open account at Threshers. They must be delighted: why advertise if you have Anna? She gives them all the publicity they need as she strides homewards, swinging those now-famous yellow bags containing one, two, three or (on one epic occasion) four bottles of Soave.

But how much does Anna actually drink? Annaholics have debated this issue at length and can only agree on the minimum: one bottle a night. The waters are muddied by the fact that, whilst the Soave is Anna's constant companion, she has other friends as well:

Red Wine

Anna, remember, is an 'honorary bloke' and the boys prefer red with their meals. And as Anna is almost an honorary lesbian as well, she drinks red when out to dinner with Sarah.

Lager

Compulsory for the boys. But Anna and Milly are partial to those bottled lagers as well and often join in the after-work ritual of swigging a quick one before (in Anna's case) getting down to some serious drinking.

In pubs, Anna doesn't mess around with girly half-pints. It's pints only – sometimes, as at Miles's stag night, downed in one. Admirable.

Vodka

Anna's halfway to doing for Smirnoff what she's already done for Soave.

Whisky

Usually only drunk in emergencies. Particularly recommended as a pick-me-up after your first AA meeting. Anna necked a quick one before hitting the Soave.

Champagne

Make use of your assets: you've got two hands, so use them. Champagne flows like concrete at Hooperman's birthday parties, so grab two glasses as you go in. On other occasions – like celebrating your tenancy – this is best drunk straight from the bottle.

A COMPARISON OF DRINKING HABITS:
MILLY: **'I had a couple of glasses at lunchtime. Always a mistake.'**
ANNA: **'Your mistake was to stop at a couple.'**

Anna played by Daniela Nardini

Television's most toasted crumpet has the gravitational pull of a medium-sized planet. A Soave-swigging, chain-smoking, drug-taking, long-legged sexual adventuress, she storms through life, scattering empty bottles, full ashtrays and crumpled conquests in her wake. She is a very tough cookie.

But she is also a dope cookie. Anna's worst enemy is Anna. Her high intelligence is matched only by her low common sense. Every time she takes two stilettoed-steps forward she takes another one back – towards the sign saying 'completely off the rails'.

Anna's impoverished Glaswegian background – 'my father left when I was eleven: my mother went to bed with a packet of Tamazepam' – is the cause of her insecurity. On the one hand, it made her hugely ambitious to escape. On the other, it sowed the seeds of self-destruction. She buys Ecstasy from a dealer – and has to defend him in court the next day. She is sent to Alcoholics Anonymous – and then gets trashed. She fights like mad to get her tenancy – and nearly throws it all away by snorting coke in the loo. But here, with a tenner up her nose and her life collapsing all around her, is the essential appeal of Anna. She's vulnerable. Underneath the sassy, brassy, sexy, strident siren is a lost little girl who wants her mum. But she can't have her. Although Anna greets the news of her mother's death with

'Pamela Anderson is but a Kraft cheese slice to the ripe Stilton sensuality of Ms Nardini'

THE EVENING STANDARD

stunning indifference, we know – and then we see – that the indifference is a façade. And when that façade collapses it's both shocking and heart-rending. The sight of a drunken Anna, weeping in a sea of spilt wine and broken glass, is one of the starkest images and most poignant moments of *This Life*.

Her relationship with Miles best defines the seething mass of contradictions that is Anna. She wants him but she can't have him, so she scatters banana skins over the rocky terrain of their relationship. One minute she is climbing into a wardrobe with him – the next she's throwing a pint in his face.

She's good at throwing spanners in other works as well: apart from doing her best to scupper her career, she almost ruins the terrific

Milly: 'I've never heard you say you feel threatened by anyone.'
Anna: 'That's because I don't.'

MILES: 'Are you crying?'
ANNA: 'It has been known.'
MILES: 'What's wrong?'
ANNA: 'I've got myself into a mess.'
MILES: 'How?'
ANNA: 'Because I'm a total fuck-up, that's how.'

friendship she has with Milly – a friendship that shows Anna at her witty, outrageous, generous, loyal and fiercely protective best. She and Milly couldn't be more different – 'I'm bad fairy. You're sugar plum' – but the friendship works because of, rather than in spite of those differences. There's no competition between them.

But there's competition in every other area of Anna's life – and at work in particular. She will consider pretty much anything in order to further her career: she samples a Sapphic snog, sleeps with the clerk, butters up the boss and bullies the opposition. This ought to make her into a monster, a rapacious amoral slut – yet because she's so up front about everything it just makes

ANNA BEING POLITE TO AN OVERNIGHT GUEST:

'I'm sorry, are we disturbing you?'
'No. No. Just pretend I'm not here.'
'Why make us pretend? We're having a private moment. Fuck off.'

21

ANNA'S OPINION OF *FOUR WEDDINGS AND A FUNERAL*:

'I mean, he had a choice. Sit in the hotel bar and drink a free bottle of Scotch with the boring git or go to bed with a stick insect in a floppy hat... The Scotch. Every time.'

her more... more Anna. As Miles says to her of the beautiful, barmy heroine of the film *Betty Blue*, 'She was a headcase – but she was worth it.'

'I don't know how she's still walking and talking,' says Daniela Nardini of her character. Nor do we. She smokes two packs a day, lives on pot noodle and pasta washed down with Soave and Smirnoff and doesn't so much go to bed as collapse in a drunken heap. Daniela professes to be nothing like Anna; friends say they have only two things in common – their nationality and their legs. Yet Daniela has found that there is a fine line between *This Life* and Real Life. 'I had a letter from a Christian who said I needed saving. She sent me three pages telling me how dreadful I was and how I would ruin my children's lives.'

Hellfire and brimstone notwithstanding, Daniela says she wouldn't mind being a little more like Anna. 'She's totally fearless and up front and has incredible faith in herself. She's a very tough cookie because she's had to fight to get where she is.' But Daniela is wary of being typecast and doesn't want to be permanently slotted into Anna's stilettos. 'I'd like to play Joan of Arc or Mother Teresa.' But the critics want more of the acidic ice queen. The *Evening Standard* 'aches to see her as Lady Macbeth.'

ANNA LETS IT BE KNOWN WHAT
SHE THINKS OF DELILAH:
MILES: **'Delilah – would you like some coffee before I go?'**
ANNA: **'Bark once for yes, twice for no.'**

ANNA'S LINE OF EXPERTISE:
JO: **'Anna's a good barrister.'**
MILES: **'She did well on a drugs case, that's all. It's hardly surprising – she *is* a fucking drugs case.'**

ANNA ON HER MOTHER:
NAT: **'You didn't like your mum much, did you?'**
ANNA: **'I should have come with a sign saying "a baby's not just for Christmas".'**

ANNA ON FERDY'S AFFAIR WITH THE PLUMBER:
'I think that's brilliant. Someone shows up to mend your boiler – and Bob's your Auntie.'

ANNA'S MOST POIGNANT HOUR:
'I want my Mum.'

— THIS Legal Life —

All the permanent principal characters in *This Life* are – or were – lawyers. And while law isn't the main focus of the series, it's always in the background. It's how This Lifers earn their money, it's often the source of conflict between them – and it's how they're going to make their way in the world.

But is it like real life? Do twentysomething lawyers really behave like our friends in the house? Is life in chambers really something of a battleground? And do sex, drink and drugs really feature so prominently within the legal profession?

The questions are greeted with a resounding 'yes' from every lawyer consulted. (Permission to mention their names was met with an equally resounding 'no'.) 'Being a good barrister,' said one lawyer, 'is often incompatible with having a happy home life. Or even with having a home life. And if you're just making your way in that world, it is important to be seen to be keen – competition is ferocious, the stress is enormous and, for junior criminal barristers especially, the money is crap.'

'There's a huge wine-bar culture amongst barristers,' said another. 'If you go down to Middle Temple (off Fleet Street) you'll see barristers spilling out all over the place, hosing down vats of the stuff. It's partly because it's such a clubbable place – a sort of extension of University – and also because alcohol is used as a stress release mechanism.'

What about drugs? 'Alcohol is much more prevalent than drugs... but yes, there's quite a lot of cocaine about.'

Sex? 'No-one,' said someone who should know, 'would have a lawyer – apart from another lawyer. Anyway, how on earth can you have a relationship with someone who isn't a lawyer? You never meet such people...'

THE ROUTE FOLLOWED BY ANNA AND MILES

Anna and Miles both gained a degree in law (the same degree taken by solicitors) then studied for their Bar exams (at Bar School: The Inns of Court School of Law) for a further twelve months. Having passed those, they are 'called to the Bar' – they are qualified barristers. Except they can't practise as barristers until they've done their pupillage – a minimum of twelve months at a set of chambers. Competition for pupillage is fierce – and the position itself is unpaid for the first six months. (In the nineteenth century pupils actually had to pay for the pleasure.) Most sets of chambers offer scholarships of around

£3000 to at least one of their pupils for that period (we're beginning to understand how Anna has such appalling debts – especially as she probably had to fund her own way through Bar School as well). During the 'second six', pupils are allowed to earn – they are 'on their feet' and have rights of audience in a court. But criminal barristers earn hardly anything – most of the work will be on legal aid and unpaid until the end of the trial and subsequent taxation period (up to a year later). Anna's debts are increasing.

We don't actually meet Anna until she's finished her pupillage and is fighting for a tenancy – the Holy Grail – in Hooperman's chambers, where Miles is already a tenant. Competition for tenancy is ferocious: Anna's desperation is believable. There is no guarantee you'll get one and many people drop out at this stage (others drop out during the fight for pupillage). Anna doesn't get her tenancy, but is allowed to 'squat'. This means she can practise there – but normally she would be there on sufferance until she found a tenancy elsewhere.

Although Anna does eventually get a tenancy at Hooperman's chambers, that still doesn't guarantee work – and she has to start paying rent (probably at the lower end of £200-£600 per month). So, like every other junior barrister in chambers, she has to keep on the right side of Jo. As a clerk, he's the interface between solicitors (who instruct the barristers) and the barristers themselves: he's in control of dishing out the work.

THE ROUTE FOLLOWED BY MILLY, EGG AND WARREN —

Milly and Warren graduated in Law and went straight to a College of Law to sit their solicitor's exams. Egg graduated in English and did a one-year conversion to Law before following suit. The next step is two years as a trainee (formerly known as an articled clerk) in a solicitor's firm. They do get paid for this – but it varies from around £25,000 a year in large city firms to the Law Society minimum of £9,000. As with pupils in a set of chambers, there's no guarantee they'll be taken on as fully qualified solicitors by the firm they've trained with.

— MAJOR CASES IN *THIS LIFE* —

MILLY'S FIRST CASE AS A QUALIFIED SOLICITOR

A disaster. Deputed to defend the wildly eccentric bag-lady Maggie Gibson on a charge of stealing a shopping trolley, Milly asks her when it first came into her possession. The answer is, 'When I nicked it, darling.' Bang goes the defence (you can't suggest to the court that your client didn't commit the crime if they've admitted to you that they did). Milly has to change her plea – and Maggie gets a conditional discharge. Anna – who would have been the prosecutor – is highly amused until Maggie looks sharply at her and says 'I know you darling. You're just like me.' Then, to Milly's horror, Maggie gatecrashes the Moore Spencer Wright party that evening, comes up to Spencer and kisses him. She thought Maggie had been lying when she said she knew Spencer. Evidently she did – were they sixties wild children together?

EGG'S MEDICAL NEGLIGENCE CASE

O'Donnell asks him to help with the case of thirty-year-old cancer-victim Macleary. Asthmatic as a child, he had been given experimental drugs that allegedly caused the cancer. Egg's disillusion with the law evaporates – this is interesting stuff. Macleary seems full of life; he doesn't look ill at all and he and Egg become friends. Then, out of the blue, Macleary commits suicide: Egg is utterly devastated and all but breaks down in front of O'Donnell. O'Donnell takes rather a dim view of this pretty unprofessional behaviour. So does Milly: she tells Egg he really shouldn't become personally involved with clients. Egg's disillusion with the law returns.

ANNA DEFENDING TRUELOVE IN A HOUSING BENEFIT SCAM

Another disaster. Truelove is too stoned to make any sense. It's his 'flatmate' Delilah, Anna's witness for the defence, who provides all the information. Later Anna finds out that Delilah has generously offered her services to the prosecution as well – as their informant. Delilah is removed from the case – but not before she meets Miles in court and offers him an entirely different sort of service in the courtroom loo.

THE SHERINGHAM CASE

One that shows Miles in good light. Sheringham is a city fat-cat accused of major fraud: the trial could last for two years and prove extremely lucrative for Miles. Yet he's unhappy. To defend Sheringham would be to sell out on all his principles: the rich, as far as he's concerned, look after their own and he could be far better employed doing something more worthy. He approaches his father (who used to sit on the board of Sheringham's company) and drops heavy hints about wanting him as a witness. If his father agrees to stand, Miles would have to plead 'embarrassment' (in this case a personal relationship with a witness) and step down. His father refuses, but later steps forward just when Miles had resolved to give his all to the case. Miles is livid.

THE CASE OF MILES V HIS FATHER

Miles accuses his father Montgomery of being a 'totally corrupt, self-serving bastard'. All the evidence against Montgomery is circumstantial and we advise him to base his defence on the grounds that the pot is calling the kettle black. He refuses to do this. The case is eventually dropped and, after taking instruction from Anna, Miles attends Montgomery's wedding where he meets his own future wife Francesca.

PEMBERTON V LOCKE

Partners in an advertising agency, Pemberton and Locke fall out and begin proceeding to sue each other. O'Donnell is handling Pemberton's case – and brings Milly on board to help him. This marks the beginning of the late nights over wine and sandwiches in the office, the dinners and the rising sexual tension between them. In the end – and in O'Donnell's words – Pemberton and Locke 'get back into bed together'. O'Donnell and Milly nearly do as well. The seeds are sown for their affair.

WARREN'S ADULTERY CASE

Warren has a client who is trying to divorce his wife on grounds of adultery – she has been having an affair with another woman. Warren finds the man's attitude of disbelief and disgust extremely difficult to deal with and, in an attempt to bridge the chasm of misunderstanding between them, finds himself obliged to tell his client he is gay. He also tells him that, according to the law, his wife hasn't committed adultery. Adultery, he explains, is 'a heterosexual act of penetration'. His client looks even more disgusted.

MILES DEFENDS A MAN ACCUSED OF FLASHING

Miles is convinced his client is guilty. Anna has a look at the papers and is convinced he is innocent: 'that poor man needs me'. She's spot on: he has an urgent need to flash at her and does so in the ladies' loo at court. Miles successfully defends his client – but is Anna going to bring charges for another accusation? No, she says. There's no point. 'All men are perverts anyway.'

ANNA SAILS CLOSE TO THE WIND

One night Anna and Jerry score some E off a contact of Egg's – Lanky Roy in Clapham. The next day Anna is appalled to find that her case for the day is to defend Roy on a drugs charge. It turns out he asked specifically for her. Miles finds her in floods of tears in the court robing-room. By rights, Anna should refuse to take the case – but how can she? She can hardly plead embarrassment on the grounds of 'I know this man, he's my dealer'. She steels herself to defend him, does so successfully (he gets off with a fine) but is severely shaken. Especially when Roy tells her they're 'in the same boat, you and I'. Anna resolves to jump ship and never take drugs again.

THE CASE OF RACHEL V THE PEOPLE (see page 112)

BECKS V COLE (OTHERWISE KNOWN AS ANNA V MILES)

Philip Becks and Terry Cole have jointly been accused of ABH, yet they don't choose a joint defence and instruct separate solicitors who, in turn, brief separate barristers – Miles and Anna. Miles tries to get one over Anna by meeting his client, Terry Cole, for a drink the night before the trial. Anna goes ballistic when she finds out – what has Miles found out that she hasn't? He's one up on her, and the trial is about to begin. Anna does some fast thinking, bullies Becks into admitting his story is 'a load of crap', forces him to admit that he only drove Cole to the scene of the crime and didn't participate in any violence. Armed with this knowledge when she goes into court, she successfully lays the entire blame on Cole. Miles is livid. Hooperman is delighted with her success and hints that they'll soon vote on her tenancy.

THE CASE WHERE ANNA LOSES THE PLOT

Anna has just been given her tenancy and is working as Graham's junior on a high-profile case of the alleged rape of a schoolgirl by her teacher. Anna is really showing her mettle and Graham (her biggest detractor in chambers) is extremely impressed – especially when she comes up with a new line of defence involving social service records on the supposed victim. Then Anna's mother dies and, whilst pretending she isn't remotely concerned, Anna starts going into self-destruct mode: she's either permanently plastered or stoned. All hell breaks loose when Graham catches her snorting coke in the chambers' loo. She's taken off the case – and very nearly booted out of chambers. The case is given to Miles.

GLOSSARY OF TERMS:

CONTINUANCE (as pleaded by Miles when he interrupted one case to take on another): An American expression meaning adjournment. More generally referred to in a UK criminal case as to 'stand out' or, in a civil case, to 'put over' to a further date.

CPS: The Crown Prosecution Service. A government-funded body that undertakes cases for the state.

DEVILLING: Anna did a lot of this – other people's paperwork done by very junior barristers.

EMBARRASSMENT: Milly had to plead this once. Anna should have done so when she defended her dealer. It's when a barrister has to stand down because of a conflict between the client's instructions (e.g. 'I did it') and the manner in which the client wishes you to run the case. Embarrassment is also pleaded when you have a close personal involvement in the case (Anna with her dealer – again – and Miles when his father stood witness in the Sheringham case).

INNER BAR: Not a pub but the Bar you belong to if you are a QC (or SILK – see below).

JUNIOR BARRISTER: Nothing to do with age – you can still be a junior when you're sixty. A barrister who isn't a QC (see SILK).

OUTER BAR (usually pronounced 'utter' bar): The Bar you belong to if you're a junior barrister.

PUPILLAGE: A period of training of not less than twelve months during which your work is supervised by a qualified barrister.

QC: Queen's Counsel. See SILK.

RIGHTS OF AUDIENCE: Having the right to address the court (barristers and solicitors alike).

SILK: You take silk when you become a QC – a position for which you apply, generally not before you have practised as a junior barrister for at least ten years. The Bar Council assesses and grants (or not) your application. QCs wear silk gowns and also possess seventeenth-century mourning dress for high days and holidays. (This outfit allegedly dates from the execution of King Charles I when barristers went into mourning – they're still there.)

TENANCY: A place in a set of chambers.

Miles played by Jack Davenport

Miles is an anagram of slime, which the dictionary defines as 'an unpleasant slippery substance'. Very apt, some might say. Others would disagree – demonstrating that the jury is still out on the case of Miles. Is he a posh, sexist, homophobic bigot with a bad fringe – or an immensely loyal friend with a heart of gold underneath the laddish (and rather luscious) exterior?

Both, actually. Miles is *This Life*'s official bastard and, as with most of the species, his sensitive side is magnificently camouflaged, lurking in the undergrowth beneath the towering ambition and the appalling arrogance: fighting against the rising tide of slime.

But Miles has his redeeming moments. On more than one occasion he covers at work for Anna – and all he gets in return is a sarcastic 'I'll call the Vatican and have you canonised.' He's also Egg's best friend and tries his (exceptionally clumsy) best to help him in his difficulties with Milly. And Miles even steels himself to apologise to Ferdy (whom he can't stand) for supposedly ruining his relationship with Lenny. The last laugh there is on Miles: cringing with embarrassment, he is manoeuvred into admitting that public schoolboys 'get confused' about their sexuality. Though *he* didn't, he adds quickly – and too late.

'Fucking fresh air. I hate the stuff.'

Miles has managed to cast off his public school background, and he loathes – and has avoided – the old-boy network epitomised by his father. He wants to make his own way in life: a laudable ambition but one that carries an inherent problem. Miles is self-centred, blinkered, bolshie and bombastic. His 'way of doing things' tends to upset every apple-cart in the vicinity. Worse, he is a hopeless judge of character – especially when it comes to women. He rushes in where angels wouldn't be seen dead – often with appalling results. Remember Delilah?

Introspection is not one of his greatest gifts, but it does gradually dawn on him that there is one woman who somehow managed to slip under his skin – Anna. Yet because Miles is Miles, he doesn't declare his true feelings to her until it's far too late.

And the fact that Anna is an 'honorary bloke' is something he finds slightly threatening. Would admitting to loving her make him an 'honorary homosexual'? Miles is distinctly uneasy with the issue of homosexuality: he insults Warren and is convinced Ferdy's sole reason for existing is to peek at his willy. We're pretty sure Miles isn't remotely gay – but we also reckon 'something happened' in the dorm after lights out all those years ago...

One supposed prerequisite for being a good barrister is to have an ego the size of a small house. Miles appears to possess a large mansion. He's something of the golden boy at work – and even when credit isn't due he takes it anyway. The only possible blight on his ascendant career is the arrival of Anna. As at home, she's a bit of a threat at work, so Miles commits the Most

'You're unbelievable! I always thought you were a complacent sod, but I wasn't doing you justice. You're actually a totally corrupt, self-serving bastard!'

Despicable Non-Sexual Act of the Series and votes against her tenancy. Unforgivable. Yet Anna forgives him in the end: it's that fatal attraction thingy. And she doesn't even boil his bunny.

Like most of his friends, Miles believes in healthy living. Tinned curries and Indian take-aways are his speciality, along with endless beers and dope sessions with Egg. He does, however, make repeated attempts to quit smoking – but his fag habit is like his Anna habit. It always gets the better of him.

Even the thrillingly beautiful Francesca can't quite extinguish the Anna flame in his

heart – but she does manage to light (albeit briefly) a cultural candle in his breast. In the early days of his relationship with her, he acquires art books, leaves them lying around the house, and utters such unlikely statements as 'Matisse thought his paintings emitted helium radiation'. Very un-Miles. Very fleeting. And Francesca *still* agrees to marry him. Must be those smouldering eyes and that chiselled bone structure.

Jack Davenport, who plays Miles, admits that while he's a 'complete twat who's going to get his

MILES: 'Why is it, Anna, that you can go round ripping the shit out of people left right and centre but the minute I make a joke I have to get a smack in the mouth and kiss arse afterwards?' ANNA: 'Must be the way you tell them.'

come-uppance' he has actually grown rather fond of Miles – 'although I hope I'm nothing like him'. Jack goes on to explain that Miles's appalling behaviour has led to drunk women going up to him in pubs screaming 'You're such a bastard!' Try as he might to explain that he's not actually Miles, it doesn't appear to work. He hasn't yet suffered an action replay of the pub scene with Anna where she threw a pint in his face, but he reckons it won't be long coming.

Jack is the only lead actor in *This Life* who didn't attend Drama School. The son of actors Maria Aitken and Nigel Davenport, he studied English Literature and Film Studies at the University of East Anglia. Then the acting bug got the better of him and he wrote to John Cleese, asking if he needed a runner on *Fierce Creatures*. He ended up playing a zoo keeper – and then immediately landed the part of Miles. And, to prove that *This Life* really does echo Real Life, he's made 'some of the closest friends I may ever have' while working on the series. They are Andy Lincoln (Egg) and, yes, Daniela Nardini. 'I love her – but not like that.' So now we know.

ANNA ANALYSES MILES:
ANNA: **'You know, they say that when a baby is new-born it doesn't really understand that other people exist and it quite naturally assumes that the whole universe revolves round it. You are that baby, Miles. You never got past the first stage. You never found out that not everything on this earth has got to do with you.'**
MILES: **'You are jealous.'**
ANNA: **'Miles. Fuck off.'**

'You've got to admire London Underground's balls, though. Whoever coined the phrase "your next train's late due to late running" is a fucking poet.'

MILES COMFORTING ANNA:

'Well, for what it's worth, I don't think you're a fuck-wit.'
ANNA: 'Yes, you do.'
MILES: 'All right, I do.'

*MILLY: 'Anna, this is Warren.'
ANNA: 'Fuck off Warren.'

Series One

Episode 1:
Coming Together

'Out there is chaos,' says Warren to his therapist. He's right. In the big bad world Egg is stumbling through an interview, Anna is storming through another one and, across the table from her, Miles is remembering, with a mixture of regret and alarm, that he had a one-night stand with Anna when they were all at college three years previously. Elsewhere, Milly is taking her first quietly confident steps as a newly qualified solicitor. Welcome to *This Life*.

Warren and Egg both get jobs at Moore Spencer Wright, the firm where Milly works. Warren is ecstatic. Egg is devastated. He only gets seventeen days' holiday a year. He'd much rather be playing football. Anna, however, doesn't get a tenancy at Miles's chambers. Hooperman, head of chambers, thinks she's a maverick. Hooperman is pretty sharp. But he does allow Anna to squat (not an esoteric sexual activity this time but a bona-fide barristerial term. See page 25).

O'Donnell is one of the partners at Moore Spencer Wright. The guardian angel of the younger staff, he encourages individuality. Little does he know. But he does know that Warren is gay and respects this admission.

Egg and Milly, who have been going out for five years, move with Miles into a rented house in Southwark. Without asking Miles, Milly asks Anna to move in as well. There is one room left. Warren was at college with Egg, Miles and Milly. So will it go to him? It seems unlikely. His first meeting with Anna at the firm's party was not terribly auspicious.*

Episode 2: *Happy Families*

Anna and Miles are prowling warily around each other in the house.

Jo, the clerk at chambers, says Anna can have her own case – a murder trial. Anna is in heaven – until Jo reveals that it's actually a fraudulent housing-benefit claim. Anna descends to hell when she meets the clients: a smack-head called Truelove and his girlfriend, the improbably though aptly named Delilah.

Warren is driving Egg mad at work with his enthusiasm and therapy-speak. The only 'space' and 'boundaries' that interest Egg are on a football pitch. But Warren is aware that there is a room to let in Egg's house and is upset that he hasn't been asked to move in. As he tells his therapist, they were a 'tight little group at college. Golden people' who didn't want him then and still don't. Egg is on the point of asking Warren to move in when O'Donnell sends him off on an errand. Egg wanders off to the park then goes home. He doesn't know why. We think it has something to do with O'Donnell's induction routine, requiring Egg and Warren to familiarise themselves with everything from the files to the stationery cupboard.

Warren's brash teenage cousin Kira suddenly appears at the office. She wants him to get her a job. Warren is terrified that she'll find out he's gay and fobs her off. Despite this, she manages to get work as a temp.

Miles was in the same court as Anna and met the scheming Delilah. She gave him an apple. Then she gave him a seeing to in the courtroom loo. Then he took her out to dinner. A self-confessed model, Delilah didn't mess about with things like food and stuck to wine and cigarettes.

Warren moves into the house after answering the ad Anna placed in the *Evening Standard*. Everyone is delighted – if slightly sheepish. They should have invited him. But Miles is the one giving the invitations – to Delilah. The first house rule – no live-in lovers – has been broken.

Episode 3: *Living Dangerously*

Delilah is causing mayhem in the house. She has a refreshingly original attitude to ownership – everything is hers for the taking. And she doesn't bother seizing the day with polite 'good mornings' but gets straight to the point with 'can I borrow some money?' Warren realises she's bulimic and tries to help her. She rips him off. And Truelove is still lurking in the background. He's being chased for debts and begs Delilah to help him. Revealing her bountiful side, Delilah steals Milly's house key and hands it over to him.

Egg begins to get into his work when he's given a medical negligence case to work on. He becomes too personally involved with his cancer-victim client and is devastated when he commits suicide. So devastated that he goes off sex for the first time ever. This is something that has never happened to Warren. He spends most evenings cruising in the park.

Miles, who has been offered a big fraud case, confides to Anna his doubts about Delilah. He backtracks when Anna tells him exactly what she thinks about his new love. Miles says she's jealous.

That night the house is burgled. The only item of any value not stolen is the TV (Delilah's). Funny that.

Episode 4: *Sex, Lies and Muesli Yoghurt*

Delilah has been through the girls' make-up, all the hot water and most of the food. Warren goes ballistic when, not for the first time, he discovers she has stolen his breakfast yoghurt. Anna plots to get rid of her – and eventually succeeds by way of a sub-plot involving more yoghurt. Warren's last vestige of sympathy for her evaporates after he offers her some malt whisky – she has already polished it off. A house meeting is called to discuss her. Very unwisely, she decides to gatecrash. Miles thinks the whole house has turned against him and makes some really hurtful homophobic remarks to Warren.

Egg's work is suffering as much as his sex life. Milly is sympathetic about the latter. Spencer, the senior partner, gives him a bollocking about the former. Miles is having second thoughts about the fraud case he's working on. Anna is under-employed and returns home early one day to discover that Delilah has been entertaining Truelove in Miles's bed. She finds a hypodermic and confronts Miles who is forced to face the possibility of being HIV positive. At the firm, Kelly the receptionist comes down with appendicitis and Kira is promoted – temporarily – to reception.

At the house meeting with Delilah:

WARREN: **'What we want is to draw up some ground rules.'**
ANNA: **'Rule number one: no anorexic bimbo blondes.'**
DELILAH: **'I'm part of this house!'**
ANNA: **'No. You are a guest. And one that's totally outstayed their sodding welcome.'**
DELILAH: **'What about Egg?'**
ANNA: **'Egg pays rent, you stupid tart.'**

MILLY: 'I just think you were a bit hard on her, that's all.'
ANNA: 'Still breathing, isn't she?'

Episode 5: *Fantasy Football*

Delilah has finally left. Miles is deeply contrite and apologises to everyone, and in particular to Warren, for her and for his own behaviour. But Warren has started to feel guilty about his treatment of her. He and Miles try to find her. Predictably, she's shacked up with Truelove and in a bad way. Warren persuades her to go to his therapist. We suspect that Delilah's not the therapy-type.

Miles has an HIV test and is found to be negative. But he's not out of the woods yet – he has to go back for another check in three months' time.

An increasingly disillusioned Egg threatens to murder the photocopier at work. O'Donnell advises counselling or that he and Milly take a break. Egg goes to visit Warren's therapist, protesting that 'I don't really need this.' The next day he resigns and decides to follow his dream to write about football.

Anna is not getting enough work and is flat broke. On advice from Jo at chambers, she dons her best pulling tackle and goes to a work party, intent on seducing solicitors who might supply her with cases. She succeeds, but only with a woman and even Anna won't go that far.

Miles realises that his fraud case is a big mistake. Hooperman wants him to go to his father, Montgomery, a city big-wig who may have inside information. Miles dislikes his father and finds himself in a terrible quandary.*

* MILES: 'If I don't go and see him, if I make some excuse, I'm going to look like a complete prat.'
ANNA: 'Oh, I think the boat's already sailed on that one, Miles.'

Episode 6: *Family Outing*

Warren spent the previous night with strange men and is late for work. Kira is delighted – she thinks he's found true happiness* and quizzes him about 'his bird'.

Budding author Egg spends all day watching football. Milly encourages him to apply for a job with the Sports Council, but he can summon neither the enthusiasm nor the energy to tackle the application form. Despite her increasingly desperate financial plight, Anna is worried when she learns that Milly and Egg are no longer having sex and engineers a special dinner to bring them back together. It doesn't work.

Kira has fallen out with her stepfather and turns up uninvited at the house. Warren is horrified – he and a gay friend are having dinner. Kira hits it off with the friend and settles down to a drinking session with them. Warren doesn't realise she's beginning to twig about his sexuality. When she turns up again the next night he is tempted to tell her but opts for the easier option of booting her out. Kira follows him to the park and catches him cottaging. She rushes in to 'save' him from the man she thought was attacking him. But there are no flies on Kira and this is her cunning ruse to make Warren come out to her. Eventually he does, to the considerable relief of them both.

Miles's father, Montgomery, knows about the fraud case his son is working on. In fact, he knows far more than he is admitting: Miles discovers that if he could persuade him to act as a witness, he would have a conflict of interest, could plead 'embarrassment' and be let off the case. His father refuses.

Back at the house, Warren's relief about coming out to one member of his family is overshadowed by the sudden arrival of his macho soldier brother Dale. By the look of him, he is not remotely homosexual-friendly.

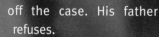

* KIRA DOESN'T YET KNOW WARREN'S RECIPE FOR HAPPINESS:

'Always use a condom, always have a zip fly and beware bisexuals.'

Episode 7: *Brief Encounter*

Domestic disharmony reigns. The dirty dishes are piling up in the sink and the final demand for the electricity bill has arrived. Anna and Egg can't pay. The former is under-employed and the latter still unemployed. He decides to abandon the application to the Sports Council and begins his novel. At work, Milly confides her worries about him to O'Donnell. O'Donnell is sympathetic.

Miles's father comes to the house to try to patch up their argument. Only Anna is at home – and she tells him how important the fraud case is to Miles's career. Montgomery decides to relent and come forward as a witness – just at the point when Miles decides to make a go of the case. Miles is livid: his father always has to do things his way.

Jo invites Anna out for a swift half. This turns into a swift gallon and they end up back at chambers having sex on Miles's desk. Jo thinks this is the beginning of a great romance. But Anna has already filed it away under 'one-night-stand'. Jo is appalled. He can't believe this, and arrives unannounced at the house the next evening. Anna coolly asks him in for a drink. The admiration of etchings is not on the agenda. Warren has a drink with Dale but finds it impossible to come out to him.

Egg quashes Milly's plans for a holiday together: if they went away now they'd miss the European Cup Final. Milly is deeply unimpressed. She makes it clear that she's getting tired of supporting Egg both emotionally and financially and getting not much in return. Chiefly not much shagging. Egg spills out his worries about his sex life to Miles. Miles is sympathetic but unsure of how to help. 'I've got some magazines you could borrow' is the best he can do. Domestic disharmony still reigns.

* MILES: **'Women think with their hormones. Well, what I mean is... what I'm saying is... sometimes they say things. No. Sometimes they have a go at you but really, deep down, they're having a go at themselves.'**
EGG: **'Why?'**
MILES: **'Well... because their glands are funny. They get stressed-out and... and they know. They know they're losing it and they get angry at themselves. So, if Milly's giving you a hard time it's probably... well, it's probably glandular.'**
EGG: **'Thanks.'**

Episode 8: *Cheap Thrills*

Egg is suffering from premature writer's block and, in between bouts of football on the TV, looks for part-time work. He finds a telesales job. He lasts four hours.

O'Donnell asks Milly to help him on a high-profile case that will involve lots of work and late nights. Milly is delighted. She finds herself increasingly drawn to O'Donnell. She is not yet aware that TV critics dislike O'Donnell, or, more importantly, that he has hairy shoulders. Later she has dinner with him but doesn't get around to telling Egg.

Egg confides more to Miles about his deteriorating relationship with Milly. Miles has a helpful theory.*

Anna is still not getting any work and suspects that Jo is punishing her. She accepts an invitation to Hooperman's birthday party. Predictably, she behaves outrageously. Jo is furious. So is Miles. They both suspect she is out to 'get noticed' by the people who matter. So do we. Anna protests vehemently that she's not an old slapper and that she was only 'having fun'.

Another surprise visitor appears at the house. Egg's father, Jerry. Egg thinks he's about to get parental support. Fat chance. Jerry informs him that his mother has been having an affair with another man and has left him.

Episode 9: *Just Sex*

Jo has stopped smarting about the one-night-stand and finally gives Anna some work. O'Donnell, on the other hand, looks like he's about to give Milly something else altogether. He feeds her the stunningly original line that he's stopped confiding in his wife. We assume this is because she doesn't understand him.

Warren has been telling his therapist that he would like a real relationship. He can't believe his luck when he meets the smouldering, leather-clad Ferdy, the courier. He takes him back to the house for a surreal experience that keeps both Miles and Anna awake most of the night. Yet the following day Ferdy doesn't answer his phone calls. In the evening Warren gets drunk and phones Ferdy at home, graphically describing the wonderful sex they had together.* He is horrified when he realises he's speaking to Ferdy's father. Later, a fuming Ferdy comes round to tell Warren to get out of his life, that he is getting married in two weeks and that he is most certainly not gay. Warren is distraught and, in need of support, later comes out to Dale. Dale is disgusted and walks away.

Jerry's presence in the house is beginning to annoy Egg – especially when he discovers that Jerry has actually written a book. Egg is all talk and little text. Depressed, he goes to the Job Centre. Not a good idea. The very process of registering defeats him and depresses him ever further. Jerry is also depressed and moans to Anna. She tells him to get a grip which, in Anna-speak, comes out as 'jump off this roof right now or do something positive.'

* WARREN ON THE PHONE TO FERDY'S FATHER (A CASE OF MISTAKEN IDENTITY):

'Hi, it's me. Hope you're feeling okay because my body's still aching.
Not that I'm complaining. I haven't had sex like that since I was at college.
Listen, why don't you get a bottle of wine and come over? If you're very good I'll let you shake my maracas.'

Episode 10: *Father Figure*

Jerry does something positive. He starts touting his novel to agents. An increasingly depressed Egg also does something positive. He applies for a job delivering telephone directories. Then, in order to revitalise his sex life, he buys Milly a book called *The Taking of Princess Selina*. This is not a resounding success. Anyway, Milly has her mind on other things – a client dinner with O'Donnell.

Prior to the dinner, Milly is jostled in the street by a rollerblader and O'Donnell steps in to play the knight in shining armour. Next thing he knows he is being charged with assault. Smooth talking gets the charge dropped. Milly can't resist telling Anna about O'Donnell's heroic exploits. Until now, Anna has been encouraging Milly's fantasies about O'Donnell. Now she's worried that they will become reality.

Miles is defending a flasher. Anna is sure the man is innocent – until he flashes at her. She decides not to press charges on the grounds that all men are perverts.

O'Donnell is not a pervert. Neither is he an adulterer. Yet. After the dinner, he and Milly come *this* close to getting down to business. O'Donnell is the one who puts on the brakes – leaving Milly depressed and confused.

She's not the only one. Egg is depressed and confused about everything. Warren is depressed and confused about Ferdy. Miles isn't depressed and confused, but he is suspicious. He thinks Anna and Jerry are getting too close. They are. They're entwined in Anna's bed.

Episode 11: *Let's Get It On*

Milly can't face either Egg or O'Donnell. Egg eventually comes out with it and asks her if she's slept with O'Donnell. This leads to a proper discussion about their difficulties and they decide to go to therapy together. For the first time in weeks they make love.

Anna is trying to keep her affair with Jerry a secret from the rest of the house. Thoroughly enjoying his second adolescence, Jerry suggests they get stoned and go to a rave. They buy Ecstasy from a suicidal manic-depressive called Lanky Roy. High as kites, they dance the night away. A bemused Warren is also at the rave. He's still upset about Ferdy – and about Dale's attitude to his sexuality. Dale simply cannot handle it.

The day after the rave Jo gives Anna a case – defending Lanky Roy on a drugs dealing charge. Anna is devastated and horribly compromised. Miles finds her in tears in the loo and gently persuades her that she must carry on. She manages to get Roy off on a possession charge and vows never to do drugs again. We're not entirely sure that we believe her.

Jerry gets an agent who's talking big advances for his novel. Anna throws a party for him. Miles's suspicions about the couple are confirmed by Egg and Miles is shocked at the strength of his jealousy. Anna is aware of this – and is now aware that she was unconsciously using Jerry to provoke Miles into declaring his passion for her. It looks like she and Miles are going to end up in bed – but we are left guessing. Roll credits, end of series.

Interlude

It's at this point that questions are asked – by producers, commissioning editors, pollsters and the public. Has *This Life* been popular? Did it get decent ratings? Is there demand for another series? And did Anna and Miles sleep together? The answers are yes, yes, yes – and let's find out.

Series Two

Episode 1: *Last Tango In Southwark*

The dirty deed was done. But now it's the morning after and there is awkwardness between Anna and Miles. Elsewhere, ferocious hangovers lurk in every corner of the house. Warren is the victim of the worst one and swears to give up booze — for ever. Jerry is stoic about the end of his fling with Anna and decides it's time to move on. Egg is relieved and full of renewed vigour. He decides to ditch his writing fantasy and become the perfect house-husband. This involves spending the change from Milly's housekeeping on scratchcards. He wins £20 — but it's the start of a slippery slope.

Warren tells the others he gives the relationship between Miles and Anna a week at most. He should have said a day: a day filled with misunderstandings and crossed wires culminating in Anna throwing a pint in Miles's face. End of romance. Anna is deeply upset but has some solace from the fact that Hooperman is considering offering her a tenancy. Miles, too, is deeply upset. Solace will come later in the form of trying to scupper Anna's tenancy bid.

Warren is mortified to learn from Kira that he spent half the evening of the party playing the Dancing Queen with 'Quasimodo', the portly, balding and bespectacled office 'boy'. He can't remember a thing about the previous night. Quasimodo can. A game of cat and mouse begins.

Unbeknownst to Milly, O'Donnell has replaced Egg with the terribly nice Rachel. Milly takes an immediate dislike to her. We're not sure about her, but we rather think we hate terribly nice people.

Episode 2: *Guess Who's Coming To Dinner?*

Anna and Miles are still doing their George and Martha act. Matters are made worse when they are assigned to a case with two defendants, two solicitors and now two barristers – Miles and Anna. Anna gets her client off by pinning the sole blame on Miles's client. She says she was acting in the best interests of her client (true). Miles says she was deliberately getting at him (truer).

Kira met Jo at the party and has decided he's worth investigating. A 'chance' encounter over dinner at the house is engineered with Warren and Anna's help, but it's more of a damp squib than a hot date.

Kelly returns to work after an inordinately long recuperation from appendicitis and Kira has to go back to being post-girl. Kira is not a happy bunny.

Nor is Milly – mainly because Rachel is being terribly nice. Milly is terribly nice back, but what she really wants to do is smack Rachel round the head. Instead she has telephone sex with Egg.

Egg takes over the running of the house and a food (and tampax) kitty is organised. This pleases everyone, especially Egg. He uses some of the kitty to bet. He's rather good at it and keeps winning.

Then Ferdy turns up. His fiancée has been informed that he bats for both sides and is understandably more than a little miffed. The wedding is off and Ferdy's parents have kicked him out. He assumes that Warren was the informant. He wasn't – but he's still mad about Ferdy and invites him to stay. Ferdy accepts – but will sleep on the floor. He is not, he insists, gay.

ANNA PRAISES MILES:

'You have all the subtlety of a rutting elephant.'

47

Episode 3: *The Bi Who Came In From The Cold*

Miles tries to scupper Anna's tenancy bid by telling everyone in chambers that she's over-emotional and will bring home problems to work – thereby illustrating that he is over-emotional and brings home problems to work. In contrast, Milly is taking work problems home. O'Donnell has overloaded her with work and she is passing her stress on to her new assistant – Warren.

Egg loses an entire week's housekeeping on his gambling. The reactions vary from amusement (Miles) to outrage (Warren) to threats of emasculation with a cheese-grater (Anna). To get back into Milly's good books, Egg goes looking for work and eventually lands an interview at a local café. Cooking, he has decided, is his forte.

Kira is relentless in her pursuit of Jo and organises a clubbing night. Jo remains hard to get – or perhaps he's just terrified. Rachel tells Kira to play it cool. Kira is incapable of being cool.

Miles's masculinity, already undermined by Anna, is further threatened (as he sees it) by Ferdy's presence in the house. He decides that what he needs is some no-ties uncomplicated sex. After a drunken night with Egg, he places an ad in *Time Out*'s Talking Hearts Service*.

*Athletic 6' barrister, 26, with classic good looks, seeks attractive, adventurous woman for fun, friendship and mutual pleasure. Do you like dining by candlelight and taking every moment as it comes? Then call me. I really want to hear from you.

Episode 4: *How To Get In Bed By Advertising*

Miles's masculinity gets its boost – he is deluged with responses. He arranges a date with the promising-sounding Judy, who turns out to be a rather dreary Sloane. Date number two is an altogether racier prospect and seems up for anything. She is. When they get back to her place it's for a jolly threesome with her husband. Miles scarpers.

Warren is livid with Milly. Spencer wants him to help on a big case, but Milly doesn't want to lose him. She can't stop him taking it, but O'Donnell can – and does. Warren thinks Milly put him up to it.

Egg starts work at the café and quickly bonds with Nicky the cook. She's a young single mum who shares his love of football. For his part, Egg shares his knowledge of Miles's *Time Out* ad with Milly and Anna. Anna composes a reply which Milly, adopting the persona of a husky, sultry temptress called Maria, reads down the phone.

Everyone is getting a bit hacked off with Ferdy, especially Warren, who stays in his room and gets drunk while Anna, Egg and Milly go to the pub where 'Maria' has instructed Miles to meet her. But Miles has already rumbled them and takes the joke in good part. He and Anna are getting on again and all is well.

But all is not at all well with Warren. Upset after an argument with Ferdy, he goes cottaging and ends up in a threesome. One of his partners turns out to be a policeman. The other man lashes out and runs away, leaving Warren to be arrested.

Milly indulges in the first of the sulky solitary baths for which she will later become famous.

Episode 5: *Small Town Boyo*

Despite Milly's efforts Warren is charged with gross indecency, GBH and causing an affray. A trial date is set and he is out on bail – but facing a potential three-year sentence. All at the house are incredibly sympathetic, but Ferdy tries to keep his distance. He is definitely, definitely not gay. He wants to move out but Warren pleads with him to stay. He does so, but reluctantly.

Warren tells O'Donnell who is, at first, all sympathy. But when the local paper gets hold of the story he puts pressure on Warren to resign. Warren is outraged. Homosexuality isn't a crime; he's innocent of hitting the policeman and the firm should stick by him. He tells O'Donnell he won't resign. O'Donnell fires him.

At chambers, Anna is helping Miles with a case which he wins. Yet he gives her absolutely no credit, publicly or privately.

Kira's sheer persistence has paid off – she's secured a date with Jo. Then she cancels it in order to be with Warren. Rather to his surprise, Jo is disappointed.

Ferdy's ex-fiancée Mia comes steaming round to the house. Miles is the only one there so she assumes he's Ferdy's lover and starts shrieking at him. Miles is utterly humiliated. He hates Ferdy, he's secretly disgusted by the Warren business – and now this. Gay life is leaving a thoroughly bad taste in his mouth.

Episode 6: *Unusual Suspect*

Alternating between depression and rage, Warren can't believe what has happened to him. The others are supportive – Milly in particular. She insists on continuing to represent him and sees him safely through the identity parade where he is picked out by the injured officer as one of the men involved – the one who didn't attack him. The CPS drops the more serious charges through lack of evidence. Milly and Warren are ecstatic.

O'Donnell isn't. The parade took so long that Milly missed an appointment with a client. He tells her she must hand over the case as the firm's reputation is at stake. Milly is livid, especially when she finds out that Rachel covered for her with the client and that the client now thinks Rachel is her boss.

Warren goes to the pub, picks someone up and goes back to his place. Warren asks what the other man does. 'Anything you want me to do,' comes the reply. The real reply comes the next morning – he's a policeman. But a real, live, gay policeman.

Anna takes over from Milly and, at the magistrates' court, succeeds in getting Warren off with a £50 fine on the charge of indecency. Warren is a free man, although the Law Society has to decide whether or not he can continue practising as a solicitor.

Ferdy tries to be nice to Miles. Miles succeeds in being nasty to Ferdy.

Nicky is nice to Egg – too nice? No, she says. She doesn't fancy him. But Jo definitely fancies Kira. They finally have their hot date.

Episode 7:
He's Leaving Home

Warren's confidence is back and he's planning a world tour. The only downside is having to break off therapy after five years. Anna doesn't see this as a problem requiring much sympathy.

Miles is the first to realise they'll have to rent out Warren's room. Ferdy is the obvious choice as he's crashing on the sofa. But Miles can't stand Ferdy. Rachel is the other contender: she keeps 'popping round' to see how Warren's doing and then dropping thunderingly unsubtle hints on the other flatmates. But Milly can't stand Rachel – especially after she wasted no time in helping herself to Warren's desk at work. An uneasy stalemate is reached.

Anna takes charge of buying Warren's leaving present – he wants 'something fabulous'. Rachel muscles in on that too and then Milly puts her foot down. She will buy the present and, with the help of the outrageously camp Paul, she gets him a pair of pink sequinned Judy Garland rollerblades.

Kira has learned how to be cool and is keeping Jo guessing. Anna isn't feeling at all cool about work – she still doesn't have any.

Warren's leaving party is mostly made up of persons of the camp persuasion – another threat to Miles. Ferdy too feels threatened – by his own feelings. He wants to get his hands on Jo.

Warren manages a final session with his therapist. He thinks he's back to square one. Yet he is optimistic as he takes his fond farewell from the house to fly to Australia and then the world. Who knows what he might find there...

Episode 8:
Room With A Queue

Miles is convinced that Ferdy's been eyeing him up in the shower and has to go. Rachel's campaign to move in is gathering momentum: Miles thinks she's wonderful (read beddable) and Anna likes her as well. Milly says she doesn't want to live as well as work with Rachel. What she really wants to do is murder Rachel. Stalemate again. Kira makes a brief but abortive bid for the room – she's far too stoned on Ferdy's dope cookies to make any sense.

They decide to advertise the room in the *Evening Standard*.*

Ferdy quietly manages to fob off several respondents, but a stream of weirdos, anoraks and other unsuitables reach interview stage. It's hopeless. Miles can't see what the problem is and goes out of the room to phone Rachel and tell her she's got the room. She scuttles round to deposit a suitcase. Milly is apoplectic. Anna suggests a vote on Ferdy and Rachel. Ferdy wins. Miles is apoplectic. Milly is thrilled and has the satisfaction of telling Rachel that it was all a horrible misunderstanding and that she's out.

Kira has been out with Jo again – but she's still playing it cool. Perhaps too cool...

O'Donnell knows he's lost ground with Milly over Warren and is trying to butter her up. Anna, desperate for work, considers phoning Sarah Newley, the lesbian solicitor she met at the party a few weeks ago. Milly visits Egg at the café and meets Nicky.

* EGG: 'We'll find someone with no baggage.'

ANNA: 'Who we don't hate. Yet.'

MILES: 'We're going to end up with a load of Bible-thumping, twitching nutters with spotty children, all moaning about Europe.'

ANNA: 'We're going to end up murdering this person, I know it.'

* MILES: 'Do you notice anything different about me?'
ANNA: 'Your spot's got bigger.'

Episode 9: *Men Behaving Sadly*

Rachel is seriously put out about the room and suspects Milly of waging a hate campaign. She tries to wheedle the truth out of Miles – but he's only interested in getting her into bed. He even goes as far as to visit a beauty salon to improve his looks* and therefore his chances with her. But roomless Rachel is no longer interested in Miles. She tells him that Anna still fancies him. Then she tells Anna that Miles still fancies her. Both are secretly flattered.

After several false starts, Ferdy goes to Mia's house to pick up his belongings. She's there with Seb, her new love. Ferdy is deeply upset when Seb sneers about 'shirt-lifting'. Seb, we learn, was the one who informed Mia about Ferdy's extra-mural activities. Ferdy retaliates by taking a crowbar to Seb's brand new BMW.

Still without work and seriously irritated by the sexist banter between Miles and Jo, Anna decides to call Sarah Newley. They forge a friendship over dinner. Anna makes no bones about the fact that she wants work from Sarah. Sarah is equally up-front about what she wants from Anna. Anna, however, declares that she's still 'partial to penis'.

Egg is secretly rather chuffed when Nicky brings her five-year-old son to the café and he is mistaken for the father. Nicky reveals that his father was actually her married college lecturer. Milly is rather sniffy about that.

Episode 10:
When The Dope Comes In

The tension between Milly and Rachel is escalating. They're being excruciatingly polite to each other, but it's quite clear that they're also trying to score points off each other. Then O'Donnell asks Milly to a conference in Paris. Milly asks Egg if he would mind her going. His reply that it's 'her decision' makes her feel that he doesn't care. She mulls it over in another moody, candlelit bath and finally decides that she won't go.

O'Donnell admires her commitment to her current schedule and then asks Rachel, who accepts. Milly is stunned when she hears and instantly tries to reverse her decision – but it's too late. O'Donnell likes the subtext of Milly's panic. She's obviously still keen on him.

Ferdy scores some dope and asks Miles if he wants to come in on it. Miles still barely acknowledges Ferdy's existence and refuses – but is happy to smoke the dope with Egg when Ferdy is out of the house. Then, when they're totally wrecked, the police arrive to question Ferdy about the BMW incident. Egg's eyes are out on stalks and he can hardly function, but Miles has enough presence of mind to flush the gear down the loo. Then Ferdy returns and tells the police he was at home all evening. Miles and Egg are obliged to support his bogus alibi. When the police leave, Miles goes ballistic. Ferdy has made him commit perjury – an offence that could mean seven years in jail.

Anna starts getting – and winning – briefs from Sarah. She's ecstatic and decides that she's going to be beautiful and successful. She goes on a health kick.*

Kelly makes a pass at Jo. Jo is alarmed.

*She buys a pot of face cream and switches to milder cigarettes.

Episode 11: *She's Got To Get It*

Kelly keeps putting Rachel and O'Donnell's calls through to Milly, rubbing in the fact that they're together in Paris. Milly is convinced that O'Donnell's rubbing something entirely different into Rachel and is eaten up with jealousy.

Kira drops her cool façade along with her knickers and takes Jo back to her parents' house. First she says they have to be silent so as not to wake her parents. Then she giggles and reveals that her parents are in Tenerife. They proceed to have Very Loud Sex – probably waking the folks in Tenerife.

Anna is cock-a-hoop about all the work being sent to her by Sarah. And she keeps winning the cases – grist to the mill of her tenancy bid. But she's irritated about all the lesbian jokes at work. Sarah is salivating over the prospect of seducing Anna. The two of them have dinner again, and both flirt outrageously.

Egg is boring on about food. But oats are not on the menu. He and Milly hardly see each other now.

Miles's father invites him to lunch and brings a beautiful young woman called Caroline with him. Miles

assumes she's just another bit of passing posh and is stunned when he's told they're going to get married.

Hooperman calls every-one in to vote on Anna's tenancy. Anna's health kick takes a back seat as she goes home with two bottles of wine and sixty cigarettes to await the result.

Miles's campaign to sabotage Anna fails. She's voted in. Miles is the only one to vote against her, but he goes back to the house with a bottle of fizz, joins in the impromptu party and lets Anna assume he supported her. The little shit.

Episode 12:
The Plumber Always Rings Twice

The boiler has packed up and the landlord sends round a handyman called Lenny to fix it. The job seems to take forever and Lenny becomes something of a permanent feature. Then he demonstrates exactly how handy he is with the sort of tool Anna is partial to and fixes Ferdy as well as the boiler.

The owner of the café, Mrs Cochrane (aka cockroach), goes away for a while, leaving Egg in charge. He and Nicky throw out her kitsch nick-knacks, decide to open the place one night a week, and indulge in some fancy cooking.

Milly is desperate to know whether Paris witnessed bonking as well as business – so desperate that she asks Rachel out to lunch. It appears that O'Donnell opened up to Rachel (although Rachel didn't open anything to O'Donnell) and told her he is as good as separated from his wife and living in a flat in town. Milly then quizzes O'Donnell himself. He confirms that his marriage is dead and that if he was going to jeopardise his position in the firm it would be with someone far more desirable than Rachel...

* ANNA: 'Now that I'm paying rent the only electric device I want in my office is one that takes batteries and answers to the name of Big Boy.'

And so Milly has another miserable bath.

Now that she's a fully fledged member of chambers, Anna wants the photocopier moved from her office.* Later she goes out to dinner again with Sarah and they share their food. Will the next course be tongue sandwiches?

Miles was adamant that he wouldn't go to his father's wedding. He changes his mind in the end and returns blind drunk and blinded by love. But who is the mystery woman?

Episode 13: *Wish You Were Queer*

Miles has suddenly 'got culture' in a big way. Television is for philistines like his housemates: he's only interested in erudite conversations about art, architecture and classical music. Everyone takes the piss – and they're all dying to meet the woman who's brought about this radical (and no doubt short-lived) change in the biggest philistine of them all.

At chambers Graham is leading a big criminal case and Anna wants to be his junior. So does Miles. Then Anna discovers that Miles lied about voting for her tenancy. Anna goes ape shit. Miles tells her to be adult* about it. They fall out as never before. Anna finds out that Sarah is the instructing solicitor on the case and shmoozes her. Sarah says she's fallen in love with her. They snog in a wine bar – but Anna can't go any further. She's still too partial to penis. And now she thinks she's blown it. But Sarah comes up trumps in the end and requests her on the case – on merit.

Egg hosts a Tex-Mex evening at the café. All the usual suspects turn up for free tequila – but miserable Milly only stays for ten minutes. Any longer and she would have taken a swipe at Rachel. Otherwise, the party is pretty eventful. Jo and Kira bonk in the back shed; Miles gets utterly trashed and chunders in the taxi home; Ferdy bores Rachel about his new love; and Nicky just gets fed up. She thinks all Egg's friends are philistines – especially Miles.

58

* ANNA: 'I'm interested to know what your definition of adult is. Backstabbing? Lying? Being totally fucking gutless?'

Episode 14:
Who's That Girl?

Miles has taken to wearing designer ties
and leaving art history books in the loo.
The others continue to take the piss — until
they meet the object of his affections. Francesca
is gorgeous, funny, clever and not remotely snooty.
She can even talk football with Egg. Anna, ploughing
her way through a modest four bottles of Soave, is
appalled to discover she really likes her.*

The case of Milly versus Rachel is revving up to
bloodiness. Milly screams at Rachel over the photocopier;
Rachel bitches to Kira about Milly being 'completely anal'. Milly
overhears this and gets completely anal about it. Time for another
miserable bath.

Jo and Kira are fed up of al fresco bonking so Ferdy lends them his
room. Jo's condom falls off halfway through** and he starts to panic: Kira
isn't on the pill.

Miles apologises to Anna about the tenancy vote, claiming he was jealous
of her. Anna is secretly rather chuffed and their rift is healed. Then Miles drops
his bombshell on the house. He and Francesca are going to get married.

*ANNA: **'Some evidence of brain activity. It'll never last.'**

** JO: 'Fuck, it's come off.'
KIRA: 'Where is it?'
JO: 'Inside somewhere.
I'll fish it out.'
KIRA: 'Oh, Christ, and who says romance is dead?'

Episode 15: *From Here To Maternity*

Cockroach decides not to come back from her holiday and to sell the lease on the café. Egg wants to buy it and, with a loan from Miles, succeeds.

Milly is worried that she might be boring. O'Donnell jumps on her and, at long last, they start their affair. Despite the fact that O'Donnell has a horrifically tasteless duvet and hairy shoulders, Milly seems happy. If a bit boring.

Anna triumphs in her case with Graham and he praises her in front of the rest of chambers. For once she's high on the adrenaline of success as opposed to chemical substances.

Miles is preoccupied with Francesca's engagement ring. The first choice* gets a resounding thumbs-down from everyone and Miles begins to panic about what to buy. Francesca, after all, is more sophisticated than he is – and five years older. He needs something classy.

Kira buys a pregnancy kit. The result is negative, but Jo's still worried.

Time for another bombshell: Anna's mother has died. The unhappy task of relaying the information to her falls on Miles.

*MILES: 'Don't you like it?'

ANNA: 'It's grotesque.'

MILES: 'I was thinking of giving it to Francesca as an engagement ring. My grandmother's.'

ANNA: 'Lovely idea. Why don't you give her her underwear as well?'

Episode 16: *One Bedding And A Funeral*

Milly goes out to see a film with an old friend (read rumpy-pumpy under the dismal duvet). Anna goes out for a drink with herself – she's becoming increasingly wobbly and has declared that she's not going to her mother's funeral. The others in the house are worried about her.

Egg's parents get back together and Nat, his fifteen-year-old brother, comes to stay at the house for a few days. He smokes dope with Anna and hopes that she'll help him dispense with his virginity. Anna has the sense to refuse. Kelly has no such reservations about helping Nat out in this department.

Anna changes her mind about the funeral and arranges to go, but bottles it at the last minute. She

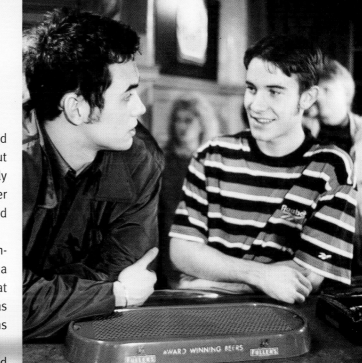

pretends that she has gone – but instead takes Nat out for a spot of 'shopping therapy'.

O'Donnell takes Milly out for a romantic dinner and then they bonk on his desk. The cleaner, however, is in the office. Have they been rumbled by Mrs Mop? The very thought gives Milly the willies.

Kira is not very chuffed at Jo's continuing terrors about her possibly being pregnant and dumps him. But she keeps up the pregnancy myth at work: anything to get out of photocopying. Milly tells Rachel to do it instead. Ouch.

Episode 17: *The Secret Of My Excess*

Anna's behaviour is increasingly erratic. She loses her keys, arrives home drunk – then continues to drink on her own in her room. Then, looking a total wreck, she arrives late at work. There's only one thing for it: she'll have to snort coke in the loo to get through the day. Graham is slightly alarmed when she starts gibbering at him. So is Jo when she tries to seduce him – again.

Rachel stymies Milly at work, leaving her with egg on her face – but not that Egg. He's too busy refurbishing the café for next week's re-opening, and sex between him and Milly is only a distant memory.

Milly bitches to the house about Rachel. Then she goes to see Warren's therapist.

‘You
should have
warned me.
I’d have
kept my
mouth open.’

Graham has caught Anna snorting coke and the proverbial hits the fan. Anna's way of dealing with it is to try to seduce a total stranger in a wine bar. His girlfriend throws a drink in her face.*

Anna returns home and Miles finds her sobbing her heart out in the kitchen amid a sea of spilled wine. He soothes her and, in the process, they both reveal their true feelings for each other. The inevitable happens.

The next day Anna is hauled in to see Hooperman. He is terrifically understanding and says she can stay in chambers – providing she goes to Alcoholics Anonymous. To Anna's surprise, Hooperman reveals that he is a recovering alcoholic himself.

Episode 18: *Diet Hard*

Anna and Miles try to pretend nothing happened between them. They both feel guilty about Francesca – and horribly awkward about their revelations. And Anna is worried about something else: she knows Ferdy saw them shagging on the sofa. Thus far, he has kept stumm.

The case Anna was working on has been handed over to Miles and she is under-employed again. Her first AA meeting proves such a trial that she needs a stiff whisky to recover.

Kira asks Kelly if she wants to go on holiday with her. Kelly accepts and realises she'll have to diet like mad to get into a bikini. Both the diet and the holiday are called off within days.

Egg's opening proves a complete disaster. So does Ferdy's visit to Lenny's sister. He's so traumatised by being regarded as Lenny's boyfriend and 'one of the family' that he scarpers and picks up a girl in a pub. He takes her back to the house. The next morning Miles meets her in the kitchen and informs her that Ferdy's bisexual. She storms out of the house. Ferdy is furious with Miles and decks him.*

Milly is mightily miffed when Egg joins her in her miserable bath.

*MILES: **‘If you're swinging it between Arthur and Martha every other night of the week I think she's got a right to know.’**
FERDY (AFTER FLOORING MILES): **‘If anyone asks, just tell them you got punched in the face by a poof.’**

Episode 19: *Milly Liar*

Mrs Mop has found Milly's watch in O'Donnell's office and Milly panics. She says it isn't hers, prompting an investigation by Kira. As nobody else claims it, lots are drawn for it and Kira wins. Rachel tells Milly she thinks the watch is 'boring'.

Everyone tells Miles he must apologise to Ferdy. Miles flatly refuses. Ferdy apologises to Lenny for running away and reveals that he's bi,* but keeps quiet about last night's pick-up. They make up and have telephone sex. Then Miles ruins everything by hinting to Lenny about the girl the previous night. Ferdy is obliged to tell all and they fall out. Anna tackles Ferdy about his seeing her and Miles on the sofa. Ferdy says he won't tell.

Francesca has declared she wants a pre-nuptial agreement. Miles is horrified – then realises that if he wants to call off the wedding, here is the perfect excuse...

Francesca, however, isn't fazed when Miles says he'll refuse to sign. If anything, she's rather chuffed: Miles's vehemence about it makes her think he believes in true love and not bits of paper.

Anna has seen Kira wearing Milly's watch and has twigged about O'Donnell. She and Milly have a screaming row about it and they fall out. Egg doesn't know why, so Milly has to think on her feet. She says it's because she borrowed Anna's knickers without asking. Egg is unconvinced.

*LENNY: 'I hope you're not one of those poofs who makes out they're bisexual just because they snogged a woman back in 1986.'

63

Episode 20: *Secrets And Wives*

Miles, under duress, apologises to Ferdy and even offers to try to patch things up between him and Lenny. Ferdy doesn't tell him they're already reconciled and lets him make a complete fool of himself by admitting to his own sexual insecurities.

Rachel is sniffing around and is now pretty sure there's something up between Milly and O'Donnell. Milly, on the other hand, sees Mrs O'Donnell coming into the office and begins to suspect that her lover is committing the ultimate sin of sleeping with his own wife. Later she sees them kissing and realises that O'Donnell has been deceiving her all along. She's totally devastated: what was she thinking of? She's lost her friendship with Anna and jeopardised her life with Egg – all for a philandering old fart. She goes home and drinks herself into oblivion.

Francesca plucks up the courage to tell Miles what she has already told Anna: she's not thirty-one, she's thirty-six. Miles is horrified: Francesca is ten years older than him. Francesca is a fossil. Miles's doubts about his marriage increase during his stag night. Anna comes along and drinks with the best of them. Later, a totally plastered Miles tells Anna he loves her and will call off the wedding if she feels the same way about him. Her heart breaking, Anna says she can't be Miles's excuse for cancelling the wedding.

Episode 21: *Apocalypse Wow*

Milly has a thundering hangover but manages to lie to Egg about why she was so upset. It's the last lie she will ever tell him. She resolves to be a better person. Anna, in her own sweet way, kick-starts this resolve.* Later, Milly manages to stumble into work to confront and dump O'Donnell. She's wildly upset and later bursts into tears all over Anna. Pleased that she's seen the light, Anna is all sympathy.

It's the day of the wedding. Miles keeps expecting Anna to step in and stop him. Anna keeps expecting Miles to call it off. It goes ahead and, as they all emerge from the registry office, Egg proposes to Milly. She's thrilled and accepts. She's so happy and confident that, at the reception, she feels she can tell Rachel exactly what she thinks. Big, big mistake. Rachel beetles off to Egg and drops some hugely heavy hints about O'Donnell. Egg confronts Anna who says it's not true – but her shocked face tells a different story.

Egg's life falls apart. He swaps his witty speech for a thinly disguised list of recriminations against Milly. She can hardly bear to listen. The wedding guests are mildly surprised but soon abandon themselves to dancing. Ferdy and Lenny abandon themselves to wild sex in the loo. And then Milly marches up to Rachel and punches her smack in the face. As a bitter cat-fight ensues, Warren walks into the room. He can only think of one word to say: 'Outstanding.'

The credits roll and we end on a 'house to let' ad in the paper. *This Life* is over... or is it?

*ANNA: 'Look at you. It's pathetic. Don't tell me you're being wild and free and having a great time because you're not. You're sad and lonely and fucked-up and so is Egg. Sort it out. Decide one way or the other. Have some fucking self respect and put us out of our fucking misery, okay?'

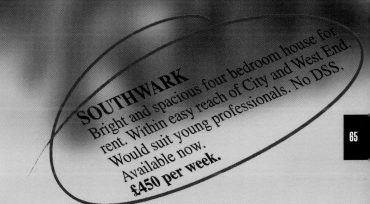

Kira played by Luisa Bradshaw-White

Every office should have one. Most offices do. The smart, sassy junior; the gatherer of confidences and distributor of home-brewed wisdom. They're perennially bouncy – and Kira is one of the bounciest. She has a style all of her own. Cochineal hair, reflective quilted jackets, Pat Butcher style shiny blouses – Kira is *This Life*'s representative of High Street fashion. (The worst as well as the best of: last seen wearing fishnet tights.)

Nothing fazes Kira. Even her first, disastrous date with Jo leaves her feeling up-beat: 'Broke the ice, dinnit?' She outmanoeuvres her cousin Warren by getting a job as a temp, and despite her lowly status as post-room girl, she's not remotely intimidated by those in authority. Almost the reverse: she knows exactly how to handle O'Donnell. He's bemused and more than a little alarmed by her.

Kira wants everyone to be happy – and achieving happiness through therapy is an alien concept to her (as is the concept of personal space). No – happiness is achieved by listening to Kira. She sets out to find Warren a girlfriend and doesn't bat an eyelid when the goalposts move: boyfriend it is then. She does the same for Ferdy – drafting in a camp disco bunny to help ease him out of the closet. Going too far is something she doesn't understand.

As for her own love life; one look at Jo and she knows he's the one. Jo's reaction – that of a

KIRA ON HER HOT DATE WITH JO:

'He picked me up. We went for a walk. He held my hand. And then he kissed me on the cheek.'

KELLY: 'Which cheek?'

KIRA: 'He treated me with respect.'

KELLY: 'He treated you like his mother. You should've shagged him.'

rabbit transfixed in headlights – is a mere detail that will be ironed out later. It is – after Kira changes her tactics from bulldozing to playing hard-to-get. Jo's masculinity is threatened: Kira has hit the button. And when they hit each other's buttons they embark on the loudest relationship in *This Life*. The only blot on the horizon is the pregnancy scare: Jo goes back into rabbit/headlight mode and Kira is really quite upset. She tells Jo to get lost.

Kira is ambitious and wants to swap the post-room for the reception desk. Her stint there during Kelly's illness gave her a taste for the job – and she was damn good at it. Kelly is hopeless – but very territorial.

But the sun always ends up shining on the Kiras of this world – and so it does with this one. The pregnancy turns out to be a false alarm. Kelly is fired and Jo comes back into her life. Bliss.

The shock news about Kira is that some viewers found her irritating – all that relentless ebullience. Luisa Bradshaw-White insists her character is lovable, but concedes that she does go on: 'I admit, though, I would have punched her by now.' Luisa cut her acting teeth in Grange Hill – and claims that the five years she spent there were responsible for all those dropped aitches. 'I used to speak real lovely.' From Grange Hill she graduated to roles in The Brittas Empire and The Bill – 'girlfriend of a rapist, daughter of a criminal, that sort of thing.' She claims she would have been prepared to kill for the role of Kira. 'It was me.' And, she adds, it was a great laugh. We can imagine.

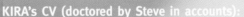
KIRA's CV (doctored by Steve in accounts):

'Bullshitting and taking the piss.'

Jo played by Steve John Shepherd

The staccato-speaking, pension-planning, permanently dazed-looking junior clerk in chambers. Jo's an Eastender (apparently *de rigeur* for barristers' clerks) and proud of it. He's a lad – and a very good-looking one. Anna thinks so too: they go out for a drink and end up having wild sex on Miles's desk. Jo's masculinity is dealt a severe blow when Anna waltzes into the office the next day as if nothing had happened. It's a long time before Jo can accept the fact that Anna saw him as a one-night stand. And before he accepts it he gets back at Anna in the only way he can – by not giving her work.

For clerks are the powers behind barristers' thrones. They're the conduit between solicitors and barristers; they dish out the work in chambers; they deal with all the money; they have most of the clout. And Jo clouts Anna.

But Jo's too good-natured to hold a grudge for long. He's all those cockney clichés – a bit of rough, a lovable rogue, a cheeky chappie – and sulking doesn't suit him. He does smoulder a lot – but that's because of his looks. Jo is definitely a bit of all right.

Kira certainly thinks so. Jo's not so sure at first – then decides to go for it. He's completely flummoxed when Kira holds back. He simply doesn't understand why they can't shag on the first date – or indeed why they can't just forget about the date and have a

'I'll tell you, I've got the battle of El Alamo in there – and they're all wearing clogs.'

shag. Kelly realises what's happening and drops some fairly heavy hints to Jo about her availability. That threat is quite enough to keep Jo on Kira's leash.

But soon they're all over each other and all goes well – until the pregnancy scare. Jo is in a complete panic. He's not ready to have kids. It's not yet on the agenda. First he wants to save a bit more; get a place of his own; trade up from the VW to something sharp... Jo runs away. Jo, in fact, behaves like a scumbag. But he's still hung up on Kira and, eventually, asks Miles if he can take her to his wedding reception. Kira accepts and Jo is over the moon.

Steve John Shepherd says he's not unlike Jo – although he reckons Jo was a 'complete bastard' to Kira. But he adds that, coming from the East End himself, he 'understands the way he acts and where his attitudes towards women come from'. Steve originally wanted to be a ballet dancer. His parents were horrified and thought he must be gay. Then, after he was 'kicked out of Ballet School for being dire' and announced he was going to act, they were convinced he was gay. He isn't. But he *is* single...

Steve will soon appear on the big screen in Michael Winterbottom's *I Want You* with Rachel Weisz.

'My mum doesn't watch *This Life*. She doesn't like to see her boy swear... or shag women over desks.'

THE QUESTION MOST ASKED OF STEVE:
'What's it like to shag Anna?'

THIS Music

Tony Garnett and Jane Fallon – respectively Executive Producer and Producer of *This Life* – agreed that apart from the title music there should be no generic or incidental music in the series. They wanted all music to come from within: from one of the characters playing a CD or turning on the radio. As Jane Fallon says, 'we wanted the music to be an integral part of their lives. And we wanted music that viewers themselves would recognise – and would believe the characters would listen to.' So there is no specially mixed music to heighten drama or create suspense. Like the sex, the drink and the drugs, it's just there. Part of everyday life. Part of real life. Every band and every track heard in the series is 'real', and the producers employed a musical adviser to help decide which character would be most likely to listen to what. He also trawled through countless demo tapes from unsigned bands for one which they felt had the right ingredients to compose the title score itself. That score is by Mark Anderson and Cliff Freeborn and performed by 'The Way Out'.

So who in the house listens to what? Admittedly, they're not always alone when they listen to music – but there are enough clues in *This Life* to indicate each character's favourite music.

Egg is identified with four of the following bands, Milly with two, and Anna, Miles, Warren and Ferdy with three each. Match the bands with the characters...

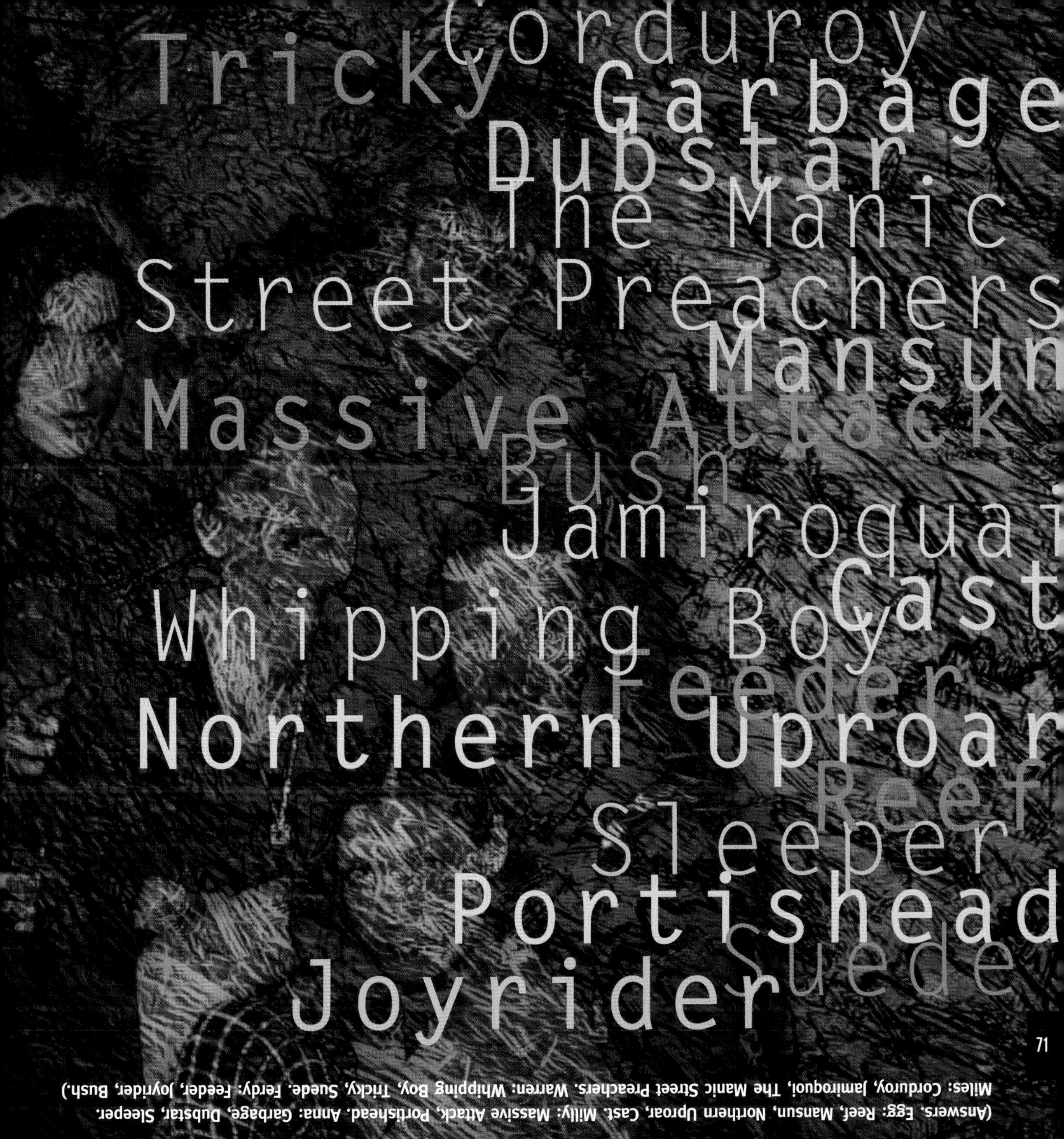

Corduroy

Tricky

Garbage

Dubstar

The Manic

Street Preachers

Mansun

Massive Attack

Bush

Jamiroquai

Whipping Boy Cast

Northern Uproar

Feeder

Reef

Sleeper

Portishead

Suede

Joyrider

Warren played by Jason Hughes

Warren: 'I'm ambitious, diligent, resourceful, creative. Keen. Impressed. Excited... Grateful actually...'
O'Donnell: 'Anything else?'
Warren: 'Gay.'
O'Donnell (smiles): 'And honest.'

Painfully honest. Warren always says what he thinks – and he's a fairly perceptive guy. His first remark to Anna is 'you don't like yourself' (provoking the rejoinder 'fuck off') and he tells Egg that he needs space and boundaries at work. Egg's response is to ask him if he speaks English.

Well Warren does speak English – but with a Welsh accent and plenty of Welsh baggage to boot. That's why he's in therapy: his repressed upbringing in a provincial Welsh town left its mark. His Achilles heel is that he wants to come out to his family. Although generally happy and confident and at ease with his sexuality, he is still trying to 'find himself' (predictably, Anna's response to that is unprintable).

Warren's successful application for a job at Moore Spencer Wright is a two-edged sword: it marks the first step to success in the big city – but he also sees it as a regression. He's back with the people who 'didn't want him' at college and still don't want him. But Warren's wrong about that: Milly, Egg and Miles just didn't know him at college. At work he strikes up an immediate friendship with Milly (they're both highly

Warren: 'I have oral sex with complete strangers. You can't get much shallower than that.'

ambitious) but irritates the hell out of Egg with his enthusiasm and therapy-speak. Then Egg warms to him when he makes it clear how hard he has fought to get out of small-town Wales and how he remains focused and fighting because if he doesn't he'll fall back to being 'helpless'. Egg is actually rather impressed – and feels guilty about not asking Warren to move into the house. He's just about to do so when O'Donnell calls him away. Warren gets into the house anyway – by answering the newspaper ad. Now they all feel guilty. But Warren's feeling great. Now he belongs.

Then his chirpy cousin Kira appears on the scene, sending shock waves down Warren's spine: she'll tell his family if she finds out he's gay. He has yet to discover that, like everyone else, Kira is not remotely concerned about Warren's sexuality. She's actually rather pleased when she finds out: she was beginning to think his reserve in front of her was actually dislike. They become firm friends and Kira resolves to find him a boyfriend – she's not convinced that Warren's sex life – cruising the heath and 'cottaging' in public toilets – is any fun at all. Nor, deep down, is Warren.

Although he's widely recognised at the most convincing gay character on television (neither a token queer nor a representative of the 'gay ghetto'), Warren never became a gay icon. *Gay Times* blames the brown pinstripe suits and the propensity to fret: *Attitude* claims it's because he 'never has any *fun*'. The latter accusation is unfair – Warren *does* have fun (being 'shagged into another dimension for six hours' by Ferdy springs to mind) and he's got a fine line in sardonic banter. But fundamentally he's quite a serious bloke on a quest.

His quest for a relationship is pretty unfortunate. Envious of Egg and Milly's relationship and even their problems – 'what are *my* problems?' he tells his therapist. 'Stingy nettles at three in the morning' – he then finds himself in a situation with Ferdy that is more problem than relationship. *Nul points* to Ferdy for being vile. Their one night of steamy sex leaves Warren feeling he's found true love – but it sends Ferdy scuttling back to his fiancée. A distraught Warren feels he's back at square one again. In need of solace, he decides, after several false starts, to come out to his brother Dale. A mistake. Dale can't handle that fact: he articulates the word 'gay', finds the word tastes sour in his mouth and walks away.

And then it gets worse: Warren's career is comprehensively queerbashed by an indecency conviction. It's the end of *This Life* as he knows it. Yet it was a life that reaped rewards. When in adversity, he really found out who his friends were (even Miles rallied round) and, on a wider level, he gave the British public it's most realistic gay TV character – and an understanding of the dual meaning of 'cottage'.

WARREN COMES OUT TO KIRA:

Warren to Phil: 'Kira doesn't know I'm gay.'

Phil: 'What's she had? A lobotomy?'

LATER:

Warren to Kira: 'I'm gay.'

Kira: 'I know.'

LATER:

Warren to the house: 'Kira knows I'm gay.'

Anna: 'Everyone in the world knows you're gay.'

WARREN TO ANNA OVER LUNCH:

'Mind if I eat while you smoke?'

Jason Hughes isn't gay – but he is Welsh. 'My own upbringing in Porthcawl was very happy,' he says, 'but I can see how someone like Warren would feel trapped and lost in the social environment he grew up in. To be gay in a small Welsh town would be a nightmare.'

Jason trained at LAMDA, where he won the Alec Clunes Award for Best Actor. He has worked in radio and theatre and in *Peak Practice*, *London's Burning* and *The Bill*.

He used to share a house in London so is familiar with all the pitfalls encountered in *This Life*.

He doesn't like yoghurt.

Dear all,
Bugger the ozone layer
– done nothing but lie in the sun for three weeks. Another three and I'll be able to pass myself off as one of the local bum boys
– only more expensive.
How's Ferdy?
Has he met a nice boy/girl yet?
Tell him I miss him.

Warren X

13 Benjamin St.
Southwark
London
SE1
England

THIS Gay Life

KIRA THE GENDER-MENDER: 'Look, this is official. I read this. It's in the safe sex bumph... There's gays right? There's bisexuals and then there's "men who have sex with men". That's what you are.' **FERDY:** 'Yeah. A poof.' **EGG:** 'So... am I a heterosexual then? Or am I just a "man who has sex with Milly?" See? I'm all confused now. I'm in gender crisis. I need a shag.'

As with straight sex, *This Life* has a 'whatever, whenever' attitude to gay sex. It's just not a big deal. It happens all the time. It's normal. Yet it's precisely this attitude that sparked the controversy about the series, provoking accusations of 'muck', 'filth' and 'complete trash'. Ferdy and Lenny's scene in the loo in the final episode caused outrage amongst those who believe that gay men ought to be behind bars rather than in them, and led to worries about the destruction of young minds. Of course those in the know were aware that Ferdy and Lenny's minds weren't destroyed but only temporarily altered by the Ecstasy they had taken. And as a BBC spokesman said of that memorable occasion; 'Yes, you saw post-coital delight, but what about it?' The *Yorkshire Post* fired back an indignant reply, implying that the young minds at the BBC were now beyond redemption: 'At one time the BBC would not have known what had hit them had they filmed muck like this. Now anything goes.'

But what of the gay characters themselves, and the others' attitudes towards them? Would they pass in Real Life? The answer is a resounding 'yes'. Warren is possibly the first major gay character in television who isn't either mincing around outside the closet or cringing inside it. And he holds a notable place in television history as the first man to leave a room saying 'I'm going to get some cock.' *Attitude* magazine has dubbed him 'The most realistic gay character on TV'.

WARREN TO FERDY (A CASE OF CONFUSED SEXUALITY):

'So what happened to you
last night? Were you taken over
by aliens from Planet Poof?
You were so confused you had a
tube of KY and a packet of mint
condoms in your jacket?'

AMY JENKINS ON THE FINAL GAY SCENE:

'I was quite surprised. But I do like the idea of him wearing a kilt.'

Yet Warren is not the reason why so many gay viewers have been attracted to *This Life*. Nor is Ferdy or Lenny: it's Anna ('she could be on the British fag-hag team at the next Olympics'), Egg ('sex on legs') and Miles ('why must the cutest boy be the straightest?') who have snatched the laurels on that one. Kira too has got the thumbs-up in the fag-haggery stakes. And according to *Attitude*, her 'tongue-tyingly cute' boyfriend Jo could have his permanent expression of confusion 'wiped by a good rogering' (and not, we suspect, by Kira). Milly, meanwhile, doesn't really feature in the gay icon department: 'for straight boys everywhere, she's the British Dana Scully; thinking man's totty, with bonus points for masturbating in the office.'

As *Gay Times* said about the series, 'It could be that the post-teen, pre 40s audience has been gasping for a realistically written, well-performed drama for aeons, and *This Life* has liberated them from the dire choice of viewing on offer. Neither the writers nor the actors insult our intelligence, which is rare in a televisual world packed with shows about pets, policemen and prizes.'

A TELLING DISCUSSION BETWEEN MILES AND EGG:

EGG: **'They're sensitive. Gay men, I mean.'**

MILES: **'That's a load of crap.'**

EGG: **'Warren's sensitive.'**

MILES: **'Warren's Welsh. Not all gay men are Welsh. And he liked to cruise public toilets. There's nothing sensitive about that.'**

EGG: **'You're so unevolved.'**

MILES: **'They like a bit of rough. They fantasise about locker rooms and soldiers.'**

EGG: **'What's that got to do with you, you posh git?'**

MILES: **'What do you know? Ferdy's probably into women now.'**

EGG: **'Oh... yeah.'**

MILES: **'That's the problem.'**

EGG: **'What is?'**

MILES: **'These bi-boys... they're completely unpredictable. I mean, Ferdy knows he doesn't stand a chance with us...'**

EGG: **'Hey! Don't limit me, man.'**

MILES: **'You are twisted. But what if he went for, say, Anna?'**

EGG: **'*I'm* twisted?'**

Warren's therapist isn't to hand to analyse the subtext of this, but we reckon it's pretty telling. Egg couldn't care less about other people's sexuality: gay, bi, straight – it's all the same to him. But Miles is threatened. He sees Ferdy looming round every corner, ever alert to the prospect of willy watching. Someone should tell Miles to stop being so insecure (perhaps he's worried about size – or perhaps he really does have a secret, shameful hankering to swing both ways?) and that Ferdy would rather thump him than hump him. And then Miles all but confirms our other suspicions: he's still hung up on Anna.

FERDY FRIGHTENS MILES:

'A woman for duty, a boy for pleasure – but a melon for ecstasy.'

House Rules

THE THEORY

1) The boys take out the rubbish every day
2) The girls clean the bath

    after shaving their legs
3) No moving in lovers
4) No nicking other people's food from the fridge
5) Loo roll doesn't grow on trees
6) Do your own washing up
7) No borrowing make-up without asking

THE REALITY

1) I rule (Miles)
2) Miles moves Delilah in
3) Delilah steals everything
4) No-one takes out the rubbish
5) Loo roll does grow on trees (it's made of paper, isn't it?)
6) No-one cleans the bath (Milly's always in it anyway)
7) There is no room for food in the fridge
8) Only Milly and Warren do the washing-up
9) Miles borrows Anna's foundation without asking

ANNA SEES WARREN DOING THE WASHING-UP:

'Oh Warren ... I was going to do that.'

House Meetings
(aka House Fights)

Serious affairs, these. The very first one was called by Anna to discuss the imminent eviction of Delilah ('The subject under discussion is festering upstairs. What are we going to do about her?'). Delilah gatecrashed the meeting in an attempt to fight her corner. Big mistake. Delilah left shortly afterwards.

How to Find a Housemate

The next fight was called to discuss who would replace Warren. Because of disagreements about Ferdy and Rachel (Miles hates Ferdy; Milly hates Rachel) they decided to put an ad in the *Evening Standard* in order to find someone they didn't hate yet. But how to phrase it? It very nearly ended up reading: 'Four twentysomethings seek fifth to share large, attractive Southwark house. Nutters, Christians, people with kids, people of either sex with facial hair and people with acne or facial tics need not apply.'

Lots of people replied to the (rather shorter) ad they eventually agreed on. One of them was the earnest Muriel:

Milly: 'I think she might be the one. She was really warm.'
Anna: 'Her feet especially. She was wearing ankle socks. I have my boundaries.'

Bye bye Muriel.

In the event they chose Ferdy. Only Miles was unhappy with that choice. We're pretty sure he wanted to add another clause to the ad: 'No poofs.'

HOUSE-SHARING:
The Best Aspects   The Worst Aspects

The Best Aspects		The Worst Aspects
You're living with your best friends	1	You're living with your best friends
You're never lonely; there's always someone to talk to	2	You're never alone; there's always someone talking at you
You can share your problems	3	Other people dump on you
The dishes are done by the washing-up fairy	4	You're the washing-up fairy
When you're shagged-out you can kip on the sofa	5	Other people want to shag on the sofa
You can spend all day watching football on telly	6	Your housemates spend all day watching football on telly
Every night's a party	7	Every night's a party
You have your own food	8	You *used* to have your own food
There's always a beer in the fridge	9	Someone swiped the last beer
You know there's always someone in the next room	10	You can hear people bonking in the next room

Milly played by Amita Dhiri

Control freak and possibly the cleanest character in the history of television. Milly's journey through *This Life* is an uncomfortable and bumpy ride, punctuated by bystanders hurling accusations of 'boring' at her. Poor Milly. She really is a good egg – she just isn't very good to Egg. Who can blame her, after five years of going out with him, for succumbing to her boss's charms and having a fling with him?

Well actually, thousands blame her. O'Donnell is a smug, middle-aged sod whose hair is slipping off his head like a duvet at night – and we're damn sure he's used to playing away from home. But he is terribly charming, supportive of his younger staff, and dangles promotion prospects in front of Milly long before he begins to dangle anything else.

There was a horrible inevitability about the Fall of Milly. She was just too good in the beginning. She laughed with Anna, had a lot of sex with Egg, was conscientious at work, flossed her teeth incessantly, stuck rigidly to her food combining and tidied her desk every day. And then Egg gave up his job and the rot set in. Milly and Egg's relationship, the one fixed point in an unpredictable world, began to fall apart. Not immediately, but gradually – and in a chillingly realistic depiction of what can happen to a couple who were madly in love all through university, who still love each other, but who are caught on the hop when something unexpected comes between them. Something called Real Life.

And so Milly, a product of the Asian work ethic, sought even more solace in her work. She could be in control there; she knew what to do. Anyway, what was the point in going home? Egg had lost his sex drive along with his self-esteem.

Poor Milly. She wasn't in control at all. O'Donnell was manipulating her all along, slowly luring her into his hairy-shouldered embrace. And just when Milly was beginning to Have Doubts, along came the terribly nice Rachel with her disingenuous smile and her willingness to please. Rightly or wrongly, Milly detected something else about Rachel: a fierce competitiveness, a strong manipulative streak, and the beginnings of a slow but steady campaign to usurp her.

From the outset, Milly can't stand Rachel. Then she can't stand herself for not standing Rachel and resorts to therapy to try to sort out why she is attracted to O'Donnell, repelled by Rachel – and increasingly ambivalent towards Egg.

When Egg begins to find his feet again and to work all hours at the cafe, he and Milly drift further apart – and Milly, also working all hours, drifts into O'Donnell's arms. But she doesn't seem to derive much pleasure from the relationship (mind you, who would?) and over-

ANNA EXPLAINS WHY MILLY IS IMMORTAL:

'You're so good. You floss. You use condoms. You're never going to die.'

83

reacts about everything from leaving her watch in his office to What Rachel Saw at The Photocopier. Her frown-lines increase, her tense hair-flicking habit gets tenser, her visits per episode to the shrink multiply by the minute – and The Baths begin. Milly is a mess. Then Anna finds out about O'Donnell and her greatest friendship begins to crumble.

Milly sees the light when she sees O'Donnell with his wife: he's been leading her up the garden path about their 'separation'. Distraught, furious and bitterly disap-pointed (principally with herself), she downs an entire bottle of vodka, suffers in silence and then resolves to rebuild her relationship with Egg. But it's too late. Rachel knows about O'Donnell. And Rachel is going to tell...

Amita Dhiri insists she is not the crumbling control freak that is Milly, yet concedes that she's got a gift for organising people. 'But,' she adds, 'when I'm alone, I'm a chaotic, blobby mess – which Milly certainly isn't!'

'Rachel, why don't we stop pretending and admit the truth?'

'Sorry?'

'We don't like each other.'

'Yes we do.'

'No. We don't. We never have. I mean I'm sure you're a really nice person but I'm sorry – there's something about you I really can't stand.'

85

'I think Rachel's terrific. She's a real breath of fresh air at work.'

Indeed not. When *she's* alone, Milly's neatly tucked up in bed, beavering away – or reading *Making Love That Lasts* in order to rekindle her sex-life with Egg. Amita says, 'Milly thinks that if she applies all the theories it will work. She can't understand how the relationship could fail if she's done nothing wrong.' Still, she applied the right theories in the episode of which Amita is most proud; the final, Rachel-walloping climax. 'She finally gets to show some feelings,' says Amita. 'She's so bottled up. And she always behaves so properly.' Not then she didn't.

The daughter of an Indian father and a French mother, Amita was born in Brighton and trained at the London Drama Centre. Now married to a music producer, she is currently doing something of which Milly would be deeply disapproving – 'waiting to see what happens next'.

AMITA ON BEING COMPARED TO *FRIENDS*:

'I'm not complaining. I wish I could get one of those bloody hair care ads, though... and the money that goes with it.'

SKY MAGAZINE

O'DONNELL ADMIRES MILLY'S PERFUME:
'I like your perfume.'
KIRA ADMIRES MILLY'S PERFUME:
'Yuk! How many gerbils did they have to kill to make that?'

O'DONNELL EXPLAINS ABOUT HIS WIFE:
'She's... decided to attempt a reconciliation.'
MILLY: 'I'd say she's been pretty successful....
You *lied* to me.'
O'DONNELL: 'My emphasis may have been misleading.'

MILLY EXPLAINS TO ANNA ABOUT O'DONNELL:
'He's just a smug, middle-aged bastard and I was his naive little bit on the side. You should have kicked me down the stairs every morning and jumped on my head until I'd realised what was going on.'

The Bathroom

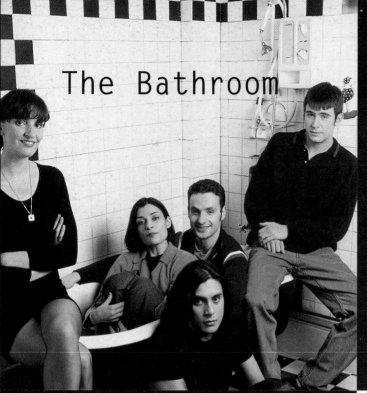

and one for the evening. Research has shown that she divulged this information to Jo in a pub, and with it a telling remark about the nature of the relationship between herself and Milly: 'I love that girl like she was my sister. But sometimes... just sometimes... I feel like doing something really evil. Like unravelling her dental floss.'

So did anything evil ever happen in the Bathroom? Well, no, but lots of naughty events took place...

Shortly after the flossing episode, Milly and Egg enacted one of the most famous Nude Shower Scenes in television history. Millions of viewers admired the matter-of-fact way the camera caught them doing what couples the world over do every day: take a shower together. The legacy of this scene was a heated nationwide debate about the pertness of Egg's bum...

One of the most famous interiors in Britain, the Bathroom is a Grade I listed building. Historians agree that while it is neither the largest nor the most beautiful interior in the country, it is important on account of the momentous events that have taken place within its four walls. Conservationists are collaborating to form The Society for the Preservation of the Bathroom in an attempt to create a permanent monument to *This Life*. So what exactly happened in the Bathroom to secure its place in the annals of history?

The first notable event was Milly demonstrating to an admiring nation the art of Incessant Flossing. She stood at the basin, niftily cleaning her gnashers in front of a slightly alarmed Anna. Later Anna was to discover that Milly's dental fixation extended to possessing two toothbrushes – one for the morning

Milly to Egg: 'I just want to have a long bath'

Later, the shower played host to Ferdy and Lenny in another nude scene: one that sparked a huge flurry of complaints. Lenny and Ferdy (photographic archives leave no doubt about this) indulged in frantic, graphic sex in the shower – *while it was running.* Mary Whitehouse is known to have penned a furious letter to the BBC, accusing that organisation of corrupting young minds by letting people believe it is acceptable to roger the lodger whilst wasting the nation's resources.

Ferdy's next notable appearance in the Bathroom was during a bout of telephone sex with Lenny. This was interrupted by a furious Anna and led to discussions about how a house with five permanent residents could possibly have only one bathroom – and one telephone.

Later Miles was to experience the downside of the Bathroom's single status: he became convinced that Ferdy was trying to barge in to sneak a peek at his willy. This prompted Miles to add a new feature to the room – a lock on the door.

Yet that lock never became fashionable – a Good Thing as far as viewers were concerned. It enabled them to witness the Bathroom's greatest moments – Milly's miserable candlelit baths. What was she doing, submerged in bubble bath, soaking for hours and sipping wine? One thing was for sure – she wasn't washing. On the occasion when Egg came to join her, he claimed he was only trying to get clean; a remark that Milly treated with deep scepticism. Perhaps Milly had already reached the conclusion that she would never be clean again: no chemist in the world sells anything to shift deeply ingrained guilt.

OTHER NOTABLE BATHROOM MOMENTS:

- Warren chundering
- Jerry sleeping (in the bath)
- Anna going to the loo while Milly was bathing
- Miles stealing Anna's Clinique to cover the bruise inflicted by Ferdy
- Lenny fixing the radiator (prior to fixing Ferdy)
- Miles flushing Ferdy's dope down the loo when the police come to visit

Egg played by Andrew Lincoln

'I love him. He may be a complete plonker but it's hard to feel antagonistic about him' – Andrew Lincoln

Is Egg a plonker? Women don't think so: he came first in *This Life*'s shaggability factor poll. Maybe they want to mother him. Maybe they don't. Either way, it's hard not to love him. Milly continues to love him even while she's cavorting with the Hairy-Shouldered One. And Egg's other friends love him, even when he begins to lose his way.

Egg's problems start when he realises that he doesn't want to be a solicitor – and who can blame him? But what does he want to do? Write about football? Watch football on telly? Lie in bed all day? Write a novel? Smoke spliffs? Egg doesn't really know – so he retreats into his shell. And there begin the troubles between Egg and Milly.

There are huge differences between Egg and Milly: she's organised and he's chaotic; she's reserved and he's spontaneous; she acts older than her years and he's almost childlike. But opposites attract – until the most important element of their relationship begins to crumble: their sex life. Egg is horrified – Milly merely miffed at first. She buys a book called *Making Love That Lasts* in order to provoke intelligent discussion while Egg buys one called *The Taking of Princess Selina* in order to turn Milly on. Neither approach has the desired effect and it only serves to underline the widening gulf between them.

EGG TO JERRY:

'Do you think I'll be as irritating as you when I get old?'

Egg's self doubts aren't helped by the break-up of his parents' marriage (probably due to his father's propensity to wear nasty Y-fronts). Nor are they assuaged by his gambling away the housekeeping, Anna's threats to emasculate him with the cheese-grater, or his inability to find work. And then he lucks out at Cockroach's café. Egg has found his niche – albeit an unusually quiet, crazily coloured and remarkably profitless one. And one that involves long hours and late nights: so Egg sees even less of Milly.

Although he does succumb to bouts of mild depression in his crisis-ridden voyage through *This Life*, Egg seeks great solace from his strong friendships – and from that with Miles in particular. For all Miles's faults (see definition of 'legion') he is hugely fond of Egg and will go to

great lengths to try to help him. Emotionally and financially (when Egg buys the café it's with a loan from Miles), Miles always tries his best – even if his emotional best is usually hilarious. He's at his very best when he's being a mate: smoking a spliff on the sofa or downing a few beers in front of the football. Without Miles to help him, Egg may well have cracked earlier.

And when he finally does crack, it's heartbreaking. The discovery of Milly's affair with O'Donnell knocks him for six, and leads to the one of the most poignant moments in the entire series – the Best Man's speech that turns into a thinly veiled, tearful and agonised list of recriminations against Milly. For Milly and Egg, *This Life* is over. For ever.

Andrew Lincoln found Egg a fascinating character to play 'because he goes on a massive journey of self-discovery. Basically he's a laid-back, philosophical sort of chap with a passion for football – especially Manchester United. But he loses his way and is gripped by debilitating self-doubts. He's knocked sideways by something he just can't deal with.' Andrew goes on to say that Egg exemplifies 'what really binds our generation – friendship.' So not such a plonker after all.

JERRY:

'Consider what your assets are. Put them to work for you.'

EGG:

'Well, I've got a degree I suppose. I could make a really useful paper hat out of that.'

'What about that thing with the trout? Can I say that?'

MILES:

'I did not stick my knob in a trout!'

Born in London, Andrew grew up in Hull and Bath, and originally intended to be a vet. Then, Egg-like, he was 'completely corrupted' by a season with the National Youth theatre and, after leaving school, studied at RADA. Since then he has appeared in three films, including *Boston KickOut*. He will soon be back on the screen in the BBC's latest costume drama *The Woman in White*, playing Walter Harkwright 'a sort of love-interest thingy'.

Little-known fact: Like Egg, Andrew Lincoln supports Man United.

Even lesser-known fact: Andrew Lincoln possesses a SMEG oven and intends to become a 'real domestic bore'.

EGG REVEALS THAT HE'S TRULY SICK:
MILLY: **'Don't tell me you don't fancy other people sometimes?'**
EGG: **'Yeah – I do.'**
MILLY: **'Who?'**
EGG: **'That Spanish girl in the Deli. I wouldn't mind going round the houses a few times with her.'**
MILLY: **'Anyone else?'**
EGG: **'Anthea Turner.'**

EGG: .
'I like bisexuals, but I couldn't eat a whole one.'

94

THIS Sex Life

DALE: **'It's just sex. Everybody's at it.'**

There is quite a lot of sex in this series, isn't there? Several polls have indicated that it's all rather unrealistic and that... there should be more. They claim that twenty-somethings are obsessed with sex. Well they are – but with thinking about it as opposed to doing it. This Lifers are no different from anyone else: they talk about it far more than they practise it. As Jack Davenport says, 'Real Life is not having sex at all, but trying really hard to get it.' Anna was (not uncharacteristically) more blunt: 'I haven't had a shag for so long I think my hymen's grown back'.

Yet other people claimed to be deeply offended by the sex. Some elements of the press cried 'corruption' and accused the BBC of lowering its standards. Aunty, they claimed, had become a porn peddler. It wasn't so much the frequency (or not) of sex scenes that offended, but the fact that they were filmed at all.

Amy Jenkins, who created the series, says that there's nothing gratuitous about the sex scenes and that 'we decided right at the beginning we were just going to do drugs, sex and swearing in passing. Have it all in there, but not dwell on it... take sex as it comes, as often as it comes.' So the sex (like the drink and the drugs) is just there. It's what people do and it's what twentysomethings are obsessed with. It's like Real Life.

So how much sex is there? Who does it most? Who has it with who? Read on...

96

WARREN:

'A tale of sex, sex, sex and more sex.'

ANNA:

'Yeah. Sod fiction. Give them the real thing.'

A Brief History of Sex

In the beginning, Milly and Egg had sex. A lot of sex. The series lost its virginity with the famous Milly Gives Egg a Blowjob in the Kitchen Scene. Many people saw red. What they didn't see was – in the words of Amita Dhiri (Milly) – 'Andy's (Egg's) lime green boxer shorts and the camera crew standing behind me.' Later we saw Milly and Egg making love on the sitting-room sofa, having telephone sex (with Milly in the office) and even in their bed. Then Egg lost the plot and with it the ability to rise to the occasion. This was addressed at some length (no pun intended) and we even saw Milly trying to coax him into action. And why not? There are a vast amount of column inches devoted to the agonising problems of male impotence and the psychological problems that cause or accompany the condition. Egg is only twenty-four. He's terrified. No wonder that when he recovered he decided to become a 'sex guru' (cue the telephone sex scene).

Miles's first sex scene was with Delilah. So was his second – and his third. All of these – with the exception of the first (oral sex in the loo at court) – were Very Noisy and prompted the irritated (and envious) Anna to phone Delilah on her mobile. The admirably athletic Delilah proved she was able to take calls at the same time as taking Miles. But Anna didn't have conversation in mind: 'Shut the fuck up!'

Despite Miles's entreaties, Delilah always kept her top half covered during sex – she didn't want her lover to see how skinny she was as a result of

Miles's next amorous encounter was with Anna – eight episodes later. So much for the serial Lothario. No wonder he had to put an ad in *Time Out*. Later he had sex with Anna again (after her mother died). But of course by that time he was already engaged to Francesca – who was sound asleep upstairs.

Like Miles, Anna is more talk than trouser. She gives the impression of having the bed-post tally of Catherine the Great – but in *This Life* she's only a couple of notches ahead of Miss Jean Brodie. Her first fling is with Jo – a frenetic and drunken encounter on Miles's desk. Several episodes later, after finding herself immune to lesbian lust, she ends up in bed with Egg's dad Jerry. Then – the dénouement of series one – she and Miles finally get it together.

The beginning of series two sees that relationship fall apart again. There are twenty-one episodes in the second series, and Anna has sex just once – again with Miles. Is this the behaviour of a modern-day Messalina? We don't think so.

Warren introduced the concept of cottaging to a wider audience, yet his hands-on behaviour is usually off-screen. We do see him looking quite sweet as he sits up in bed sipping post-coital champagne with an off-duty policeman, but his Very Noisy Night with Ferdy is his only graphic on-screen exploit.

It's Ferdy who brings more graphic gay sex to the screen. His one, filmed, heterosexual encounter apart (the one that prompted him to punch Miles), he's seen in Lenny's bed, then in The Famous Shower Scene

wedding. It was this last scene that provoked the strongest cries about falling standards, 'tasteless trash', 'muck' and 'filth'.

No-one complained about Kira and Jo having sex – maybe because viewers had to wait so long for it to happen. Kira surprised herself (and alarmed Jo) by playing cool, kept him on the boil for several episodes and finally let him have his wicked way – in episode eleven of series two. After that they make up for lost time: both of them live with their parents so whenever there's a chance for a quickie they take it.

The only other person to get her kit off (and boy has she been waiting for an opportunity), is Kelly. She seduces Egg's younger brother Nat, allaying his fears with the one of the most unlikely pieces of dialogue in *This Life*.*

*'It's okay, I'm a virgin too.'

Safe Sex

It's not in your face (as it were), but it's always mentioned and it's always practised. The only exception is Miles and Delilah. Miles admits to Warren that they didn't use protection – a huge risk given that Delilah is both sexually promiscuous and possibly a user. Even if she's not a heroin addict then her other love – Truelove – most certainly is: Anna found the hypodermic he left in Miles's bedroom.

Miles is terrified. He goes for an HIV test and is relieved that he's in the clear – but he has to go back for another in three months' time. He does. Clear again. And although the risks he took are never mentioned again, he's learned his lesson.

Everyone else – including Milly and Egg who have been together for five years – uses condoms. Like sex itself, the issue of safe sex is part of *This Life* – because it's part of Real Life.

Baring All In Front Of The Camera:

AMITA DHIRI: **'I found the nudity absolutely terrifying. I had to get my kit off on the second day.'**

LUISA BRADSHAW-WHITE (KIRA) ON THE STEAMY SEX SCENE WITH JO THAT WAS HEARD IN AUSTRALIA: **'Did you notice we were actually fully clothed during that? Steve and I were the only two that had a nudity clause.'**

JACK DAVENPORT: **'It might have more nudity than Kavanagh QC, but I'm not sure people would like to see John Thaw doing naked love scenes.'**

DANIELA NARDINI: **'I'd rate a nude scene the same as a trip to the dentist, and I hate the dentist.'**

'Ms Nardini's mother must have been worried about her daughter catching pneumonia, so much time did she spend with her kecks off.' THE INDEPENDENT

JACK DAVENPORT: **'As far as erotic experiences go, it's up there with being mugged.'**

ANDREW LINCOLN: **'I have a pert bum? I wouldn't know. I don't see it that often. It's behind me, you know.'**

Who's Slept With Who

MILES: Delilah, Anna and Francesca
ANNA: Miles, Jo and Jerry
EGG: Milly
MILLY: Egg and O'Donnell
FERDY: Mia, Warren, Lenny, an unnamed man and a one-night (female) stand
JO: Anna and Kira
KIRA: Jo
KELLY: Nat
WARREN: Figures unavailable at time of going to press

Sex Talk

FERDY: **'What kind of sex are you after?'**
ANNA: **'Frequent.'**

EGG TO MILLY: **'Sucking any part of your love monster's body is foreplay.'**

ANNA RE SEX: **'Well if I'm so bloody hot at it then why do I spend most of my nights with a bottle of Soave, Tolstoy and a frozen pasta?'**

ANNA: **'The longest relationship I ever had lasted three months.**
This army guy. He was posted to Gibraltar.
Only had two weekends' leave the whole time.'

MILES: **So you're going to bugger-up my chances with other women, now?'**
ANNA: **'Are you really going to need any help with that?'**

MILES: **How would you like it if I got you a haggis for your birthday?'**
ANNA: **'If it was a statement about my sexuality I'd be fairly alarmed.'**

ANNA ANALYSES KISSING: **'Sometimes you go straight for the kiss and it's "wallop" – straight to the groin. You forget what they look like. Until the next morning.'**

ANNA TO FERDY AND LENNY: **'You've got a way of making romance sound like a horrific perversion – which it is, of course. You want my advice? Stick to meaningless shagging. You always know where you are.'**

Ferdy played by Ramon Tikaram

This Life's spokesman for Equal Opportunities, the biker in black bats for both sides. Rampant, monosyllabic and grumpy, with big hair and big hangups, Ferdy blow dries his boxers and batters BMWs with pieces of scaffolding. Confused? So is Ferdy.

But it's not funny to make fun of Ferdy, for Ferdy spends his life being tortured whenever he has any fun. It's easy for the others (with the glaring exception of Miles) to be comfortable with his bisexuality, but Ferdy is in agonies about it: it's just something he can't accept. He regards it as the source of all his troubles.

He's probably right. He first appears on the screen as Warren's Big Hope. After one night of rampant sex Warren is babbling to his therapist about how Ferdy's 'the one'; about how he can see himself taking Ferdy back to the valleys to meet the folks. But Ferdy ignores Warren's phone calls and is still intent on getting married to Björk look-alike Mia in two weeks' time. Warren is distraught – and so is Ferdy when Mia finds out about the extra-mural activities. Ferdy thinks Warren told her and it's not until much later he discovers the informant was Seb, an ex-colleague who proceeds to take Ferdy's place in Mia's life. By way of thanks Ferdy proceeds to take a scaffold pole to Seb's BMW.

And that's not even the half of it. After Warren is caught cottaging, he implores Ferdy to

FERDY'S CHAT-UP LINE TO LENNY:

'I think my wall-socket's loose.'

102

keep him company in the house – platonically. Even though he has been kicked out of his parents' home, Ferdy is reluctant to stay. He's extremely uncomfortable around Miles, and the house is not a happy place to be at the moment. Yet Ferdy is still crashing there after Warren's departure – and he wants to take Warren's place. Why? Because he's made some friends, that's why. Like Warren, he wants to belong somewhere, and he's bonded with Anna, Milly – and especially Egg. Miles won't admit it, but he's ferociously jealous of Egg's friendship with Ferdy. In his quiet way, Ferdy becomes the catalyst for Egg's career as a cook, teaching him Mexican recipes and, more importantly, boosting his confidence.

Sex remains a problem: he's started an affair with Lenny the plumber but still can't handle the idea of having a boyfriend – especially when Lenny introduces him to his sister. Next thing Ferdy knows he's picked up a girl and taken her back to the house for the night. A big mistake: Miles finds out and informs her of Ferdy's batting tactics and, when Ferdy and Lenny get back together, drops

hefty hints to the latter about the same issue. Ferdy loses it and thumps Miles: 'just tell them you got punched in the face by a poof'. It's the mortification of Miles.

What Miles doesn't know is that Ferdy saw what was going down on the sofa while the newly affianced Francesca was asleep upstairs. He could have blown the whistle, but he didn't – and never does. Ferdy may be confused, but he isn't spiteful.

He tries, again and again, to form some sort of friendship with Miles – but Miles is having none of it. The homophobic taunts flow thick and fast and he refuses to have drinks with Ferdy or even to share his dope – in his presence at least. When Ferdy is out of the house it's a different story and, on the night when the police come to quiz Ferdy about the BMW incident, Miles is getting wrecked with Egg on Ferdy's blow. Egg gets the giggles in front of the plod and is in such a mess he can't even make tea. Miles rages around, flushes Ferdy's dope down the loo – and then finds himself having to commit perjury 'to cover Ferdy's arse'. A splendid irony.

Eventually Miles and Ferdy make peace

LENNY'S SISTER REVEALS ALL:

'Lenny's told me nothing about you whatsoever - apart from the size of your genitals.'

– and Ferdy and Lenny make frantic love in the loo at Miles's wedding. Ferdy declares his love for Lenny – but somehow we reckon the story of Ferdy's sexual struggles hasn't ended...

Ramon Tikaram has never had sex with a man. 'I feel really bad about that,' he says. 'Somehow I feel it means I'm not justifying my existence as Ferdy.' Ferdy probably wouldn't mind: Ramon's scenes with Warren and later with Lenny look pretty convincing – but Ramon himself wouldn't know: 'I've never watched my sex scenes in the show. I just can't. I can shag a man in a scene – no problem. But watching myself do it, that's quite different.'

Born of a Fijian Indian Officer in the British Army and a mother from the Sarawak rain forest, Ramon grew up in – yes, you've guessed it – Dover. He hated the place.

Ramon wanted to be an actor from an early age and applied to the National Youth Theatre. He went on to university and to a degree in English – and then back to acting. Ferdy hasn't been his only leather-clad character, he played a trendy pirate in the film *Cutthroat Island*. Ramon is also a musician. It runs in the family: his younger sister is the singer Tanita Tikaram.

LITTLE KNOWN FACT: Ferdy is the only Mexican who doesn't know the words to La Bamba.

MILES WARMS TO FERDY:
'Do we really need another poof clogging up the fridge with politically correct yoghurt?'
ANNA: **'He's bisexual, actually.'**
MILES: **'So none of us are safe.'**

105

'i just feel... well... used.'

'Used?'

'Yes. Used and abused. They don't care about me. All they care about is themselves. Themselves; their drink and their drugs. They drink and take drugs all over me. And have sex. it's the sex that really bothers me.'

'And so you would like to talk about it?'

'if i could ever get a word in edgeways, yes.'

'I'm detecting some anger here...'

'... that's because i'm angry.'

'... you were telling me about being bothered by sex. Shall we explore that a little more?'

'*i'm* not bothered by sex. *They* are. First it was Jerry. Don't get me wrong — i have nothing against him... but i draw the line at having nasty Y-fronts draped all over me...'

'Yuk!'

'Precisely. But when he finally got it together with Anna they decamped to her room. Then things were all right until... until Milly and Egg had sex.'

'On you?'

'Yes.'

'Oh. And then...?'

'Well, they didn't do it again — Milly got anal about being seen from the street. But Anna and Miles had no such qualms.'

'I thought Miles was engaged to Francesca?'

'He was. Now he's married to her. But he had sex with Anna on me.'

'Really! A classic instance of the transgression of social norms.'

'And what's more Ferdy saw it all.'

'I thought Ferdy was crashing on you?'

'No, that was before. And while he was crashing he slept with Warren.'

'On you?'

'Yes. But chastely.'

'So that's OK then? I'm OK, you're OK?'

'No i'm not OK! Nat came to stay.'

'But I thought Nat shagged Kelly in one of the bedrooms?'

'How did you know that?'

'Um... well, I happen to be the therapist to most of the house. Word gets around you know.'

'Not from Anna?'

'No. She's very anti-therapy.'

'i'm beginning to realise why. i'm paying through the nose and i haven't even begun...'

'Shall we begin at the next session? I'm afraid your time's up.'

The Invisible Shrink

We never see her; her name (Elaine) is only mentioned once; and her disembodied voice soothes whilst gently probing into the problems of Warren, Milly and Egg. Warren talks freely and easily – he's been a client for five years – and while he's not a 'victim' of therapy, he does rely heavily on it. Yet it's something new for Egg and Milly and their visits, for us as well as for the therapist, are telling in what they don't say to her.

Egg goes against his will which, like Anna's being forced to attend Alcoholics Anonymous (and Delilah being dragged kicking and screaming to Elaine) is a recipe for resistance, if not disaster. Egg squirms in the chair, insists that 'I don't really need this' and that 'everything's fine'. Protesting too much? We think so. We know so. Egg has had an easy life up till now – when it starts going wrong he simply doesn't know what to do. And he's most reluctant to share his problems with a complete stranger. It's when he goes to see Elaine with Milly that he suddenly reveals the extent of his love for Milly – and his secret worries about her: 'If you have a relationship with another man whilst you're going out with me – then it's over.' Milly is rather touched – and torn.

When Milly starts going on her own – secretly – she maintains the façade that her worries are exclusively about Egg. Elaine knows better. Milly mentions 'my boss' twice in one sentence during her first session. Later, through Elaine's eyes, we see Milly's own eyes light up every time she mentions O'Donnell, and darken as she utters the dread word 'Rachel'. And as Milly's visits become more frequent, so does her self-knowledge. She realizes she wants to get caught out in her affair so that she'll be forced to make a decision. The bitter irony is that she does make a decision – and then gets caught out.

But therapy has its detractors, and chief amongst them is Anna.

Here she is intercepting Elaine's phone call to Warren:

'Hello, it's Anna. I'm sure you've heard a lot about me, central figure in Warren's life that I am. Less a friend, more an icon really.'

(Anna listens as Elaine wonders if Warren's all right – he stood her up on their last appointment. Anna sees red):

'Oh *did* he? Well he's not topped himself if that's what you're worried about – in fact he seems on top form. I don't know where he is... well excuse me I don't agree. He didn't stand you up, he missed an *appointment*. You're not a friend, you're getting paid. Deal with it.'

(Anna slams down the phone and turns to the others – amongst them a shell-shocked Warren):

Anna: 'Well, this calls for a celebration. Warren has finally exited the womb. Miles, you hold him upside down while I smack his bottom.'

Warren: 'You didn't have to speak to her like that.'

Anna: 'I was doing you a favour. her sort never let go. She'd have you phoning in from Australia.'

She does have a point: Warren feels he can't leave the country without finishing, or at least interrupting his therapy. He's been dithering desperately about it.

But then Warren also has a point:

'Why is it, Anna, the people who are most hostile towards therapy are – coincidentally – also the ones with most to gain? Funny that.'

So, yet again, *This Life* reflects Real Life. Therapy is a highly controversial issue.

109

Rachel played by Natasha Little

A minx or a sphinx? There's no doubt about it: Rachel is a riddle. She glides in silence through the office, her face an inscrutable mask. Her suits are sober; her make-up perfect; her eyes watchful. She is blonde. She is clever, polite and ambitious. But there is *something* about her. And then, suddenly, you realise what it is – her hair is too expensive for a trainee solicitor. Either she has stapled it to her head or someone 'does' it every morning. Suspicious.

But everybody likes Rachel. She's fun-loving, drinks a lot, smokes in the loo at work and gets pally with Kira. Anna thinks she's great. Miles thinks she'd be a great shag. O'Donnell thinks she's marvellous. She's the perfect contender for the spare place in the house when Warren leaves. But there is a problem – Milly hated her on sight. From the first we all knew that they would never see eye to eye. It's not just that Rachel is Egg's replacement and O'Donnell didn't tell Milly about her appointment; it's something indefinable. Miles would say it's something hormonal. And poor Rachel just can't get it right. She tries too hard. She tries to please. She is so eager to impress Milly that she has the opposite effect.

Or does Rachel have a different agenda altogether? Is she trying to usurp Milly in O'Donnell's good books – and in his bed? For let there be no doubt – Rachel knows. She hasn't spent all that time lurking by the photocopier for nothing. Rachel never misses a trick. She goes to the conference in Paris with O'Donnell. That's Milly's fault – but she holds it against Rachel. And she suspects that 'something happened'. Something did – Rachel and O'Donnell developed a friendship that excluded Milly.

Rachel may try too hard to manoeuvre herself into the house, but we can't help feeling sorry for her when, after Miles tells her the room is hers (because he wants to shag her), Milly tells her it was all a mistake (because she can't stand the sight of her). It was indeed a mistake, but poor Rachel only wants to belong, to escape from living

with her dreadful mother. Then doubt sets in again... a dreadful mother? Ominous.

It's not until the wedding that we finally get to grips with Rachel. Only then do we get a real sense that she's hell-bent on ruining Milly – and up to the last she plays her cards so cleverly that she leaves an element of doubt in our minds. But not in Milly's mind. Milly's right hook – one of the most dramatic punches in television history – lands smack on Rachel's chin.

'Rachel,' says Natasha Little, 'is just one of those people. I've met them. You just don't like them. There's something about them.' Yet Natasha claims Rachel isn't dreadful – just horribly insensitive. Rachel is the second insensitive blonde Natasha has played on television (she was Jenny in *London's Burning*), though blondness is the only characteristic she shares with those other women. And even that might disappear: 'I'd chop my head off for the right part.'

A graduate of the Guildhall School of Drama, Natasha will appear in Granada's forthcoming *Far From The Madding Crowd* in which she plays Fanny who has a horrible time, gets pregnant and ends up in a workhouse. A fate that Milly would love to befall Rachel.

RACHEL PITCHES FOR THE SPARE ROOM:
(TO MILLY): **'You don't really get to know someone till you've lived with them, do you?'**

RACHEL PITCHES EVEN HARDER:
(TO EVERYONE): **'Well, I hope you'll be considering me. Outgoing single female who's out a lot and loves to clean.'**

RACHEL MAKES MILLY'S BLOOD BOIL:

'Shame O'Donnell went home. He gets quite frisky after a few drinks. Really lets his hair down.'

The Case Of RACHEL

VERSUS

THE PEOPLE

THE ACCUSATION:

Rachel is a scheming bitch

THE PLEA:

Not Guilty

COUNSEL FOR THE DEFENCE:

O'Donnell

COUNSEL FOR THE PROSECUTION:

Milly

The Argument For The Defence

- Rachel has no time to scheme – she spends all her time working.
- She gets in even earlier than Milly, who has been deputed to 'look after' her.
- Rachel isn't afraid to voice an opinion – she disagreed with Milly over a sexual harassment case – but will apologise if she is in the wrong.
- She is helpful, fun and good in a crisis – she came to Milly's rescue when she was late for a client and dealt admirably with his claim for industrial injury.
- She has a stillness and great depth.
- She often works late: one night O'Donnell came to chat and she was so tired she nearly fell off her chair.

- Rachel is very observant. Nothing escapes her eagle eye.
- She didn't let on that Warren was late because of a hangover, rather than food poisoning.
- She doesn't stand on ceremony and is more than happy to do menial tasks such as photocopying.
- She's one of the girls and even goes out to lunch with Kira.
- She gets on very well with Milly's housemates.

- She is very nice to O'Donnell.
- She confided in Egg her concern for Milly's well-being, and suggested Milly might be upset after a row with O'Donnell.

The Argument For The Prosecution

- Rachel spends all her time at work scheming.

- She gets in even earlier than Milly in order to try to get one over on her.
- She tried to muscle in on – and nearly scuppered – Milly's sexual harassment case.

- She let another client believe she was Milly's boss when she took advantage of Milly's absence in an industrial injury case.
- Still waters run deep.
- She has ulterior motives for working late: one night O'Donnell came to chat and she stretched backwards, showing him her midriff.
- Rachel is extremely nosey. Nothing escapes her beady eye.
- She told O'Donnell that Warren was late because of a hangover and not food poisoning.
- She's always standing by the photocopier, from where she can get a bird's eye view of the entire office.
- She goes out to lunch with Kira and plants notions of an affair between Milly and O'Donnell.
- She brown-noses Milly's housemates when she learns there's a room up for grabs.
- She is very nice to O'Donnell.
- She deliberately went out of her way to seek out Egg, leaving him in no doubt that Milly had been having an affair with O'Donnell.

The Summing Up For The Defence:

Rachel finds Milly difficult and their relationship is fraught with misunderstandings. She suspects Milly may even be jealous of her (had she been able to witness Milly trying 'a Rachel' in front of her bedroom mirror, she would have been more than suspicious). Rachel means well and always tries to do the right thing, but often says the wrong thing. Rachel may be insensitive – but she is not a scheming bitch.

The Summing Up For The Prosecution:

When Milly came storming up to the Accused at Miles's wedding, the Accused screamed 'It wasn't me!' before she had even been informed of the accusation. I rest my case.

The Jury:

Phil (Warren's friend). Mrs Cochrane (ex-owner of the café). Cora (the swinger who answered Miles's Talking Hearts ad). Paul (the camp disco bunny drafted in to help Ferdy come out). Dale (Warren's macho brother). Caroline (Miles's new step-mother). Tom McGregor (author of this book). Mia (Ferdy's ex-fiancée). Nicky from the café. One of Kelly's trolls. Francesca. Seb (Mia's new squeeze).

The (UNANIMOUS) Verdict:

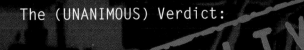

GUILTY

Lenny played by Tony Curran

The gay plumber lends an entirely new meaning to U-Bend. Indeed he could be the inspiration for quantities of bad jokes about push-fit joints, flexible connectors, rim-supply bidets and ballcocks. Instead the poor boy becomes the butt of household jokes. Much worse.

Lenny comes to mend the boiler and, as Anna put it 'Bob's your Auntie' – next minute he's in bed with Ferdy. Little does he know it's a bit like being in bed with Madonna – you never know what's going to happen next. It's not long before he learns that Ferdy runs hot and cold quicker than any shower and that he's 'not gay'. Three of the steamiest scenes in the series (one of them, fittingly, in the shower) suggest otherwise.

The rest of the house is unfazed by the idea of Ferdy having a boyfriend. Kira is ecstatic. It's Ferdy himself who is totally freaked by the idea: so freaked that he does a runner at the idea of meeting Lenny's mother.

Happily, Lenny gets his man in the end: he turns up at Miles's wedding reception wearing a kilt (presumably for easy access) and, with the help of a few Es, he and Ferdy get down to business in the bog, outraging Outraged of Tunbridge Wells in the process. But Lenny doesn't care. He seems to have shifted Ferdy's gear stick into permanent gay mode, and even provokes a declaration of love from his red hot Mexican chili. Sweet.

FERDY ON MILES'S WILLY:

'It weren't that great.'

LENNY: 'That's a shame. I kind of picture Miles with a wonger the size of my arm.'

O'Donnell played by David Mallinson

We just didn't like him, did we? Was it the slightly-too-long receding hair or the voice that just never wavered from that quiet, caring monotone? Even when Milly stormed into his office to confront him about his infidelity (he was sleeping with his wife all along), he remained calmly smug. 'My emphasis,' he declared of his marital situation, 'may have been misleading.'

But Milly apart, he did seem to genuinely care about his trainees in the office – even if he did tend to spout 'management speak'. No doubt he hadn't really thought about all the implications behind 'We don't encourage distinctions between your real self and your work self'. How was he to know that Egg was a ditherer and Warren a cottager? And he probably didn't have much choice about sacking Warren.

And he did try to be fun – he just wasn't very funny. He once told a witty story to Rachel and Milly. Rachel managed a hollow laugh. Milly just walked away.

Like thousands of other businessmen, O'Donnell was really married to his work. And marriage, after all, is supposed to include sex – so in a way he wasn't unfaithful after all. Milly was just unfortunate.

Nicky played by Juliet Cowan

Every day's a bad hair day for the girl in the caff. Will she be wearing those bunches, or will she tease her tresses into that troll-like top-knot? Viewers are divided as to which style is least becoming. But her hair apart, Nicky's a sweetie – and Egg's saviour. If she hadn't put in a good word for him at Cochrane's café, he would never have found his true vocation.

Egg's the one who does all the complaining in the café – but Nicky has good reason to complain about her own life. Pregnant at nineteen by a college lecturer who scarpered, she is a single mother to the five-year old George, the boy who nearly ruined Anna's reputation. She was found reading him a bed-time story – at his request. George also had an effect on Egg: he made him broody. Milly was highly disapproving about that. She's very firmly of the opinion that you plan these things well in advance – something she rather tactlessly told Nicky.

Nicky herself thinks Milly doesn't know how lucky she is with Egg, and tells her as much. 'He wanted to name one of the recipes after you, you know.' Milly is rather touched – until Egg tells her the recipe was going to be called 'Milly's Mutton Chops.'

THE QUESTION MOST ASKED OF JULIET:
'You're off that show, incha? The one where the poofs kiss.'

Kelly played by Sacha Craise

The nail-filing, troll-collecting, food-loving receptionist at Moore Spencer Wright. Work is a necessary evil to Kelly and her appendicitis was a blessing in disguise: 'complications' set in and she was obliged to take the longest convalescence in history. Kira took her place and when she returned – having told Kira she had got another job – a furious row ensued. O'Donnell later gave her a written warning for 'abusing her position' (little did he know that she had eavesdropped on Milly's telephone sex with Egg).

Many people felt that Kelly abused her position from the very beginning. Her desk is the company's 'front line' – so how come she's allowed to keep those ghastly trolls on it if O'Donnell's so worried about the company's image? Still, the trolls are a vehicle for prising information out of Kelly: 'Tell or I'll cut off their hair'. Kelly tells.

KIRA ON KELLY'S APPENDIX SCAR:

'Could be anything. Someone probably harpooned you by mistake.'

Francesca played by Rachel Fielding

The Perfect One. She's clever, funny, gorgeous and popular. Everyone in the house has been dying to meet the mysterious girl who has had such a dramatic effect on Miles. But Miles is wary of introducing her to his mates: what will the older, more sophisticated art- and opera-loving Francesca make of his philistine friends? And what will acid-tongued Anna, mistress of the punishing put-down, say to her?

Miles should have had more faith in his new girlfriend – and in his housemates. Francesca floats into the house and has everyone eating out of her hand in a matter of minutes. Even Anna's initial attempts to resist are futile. Miles, of course, is mortified that Egg and Ferdy are noisily engaged in a game of Subbuteo when she arrives. Egg and Ferdy are slightly mortified as well. It would have looked better, somehow, if they had been discussing Bach's partitas and sonatas, or abstract art.

Except that it wouldn't. Francesca is a football fan. Francesca is all things to all women and all men. And she's not just going out with Miles – she's already engaged to him.

FRANCESCA AFTER MILES BONKED ANNA:

'Is she all right? What was wrong?'

MILES: 'She's just fucked-up.'

FRANCESCA: 'Did you manage to unfuck her ... as it were?'

MILES: 'Sort of.'

FRANCESCA: 'Well done.'

118

Anna wants to hate her but can't – and then feels terribly awkward when Francesca begins to confide in her. Francesca senses something's wrong with Miles and thinks it's the fact she's five years older than him. Anna says that's rubbish. Then Francesca drops her bombshell – she's actually thirty-six, ten years older than Miles. Then Miles too begins to confide in Anna. He's worried he's rushing into the marriage. He's unhappy about the pre-nuptial agreement Francesca is insisting on.

Anna's beginning to feel like a pig in the middle – and not a very happy pig. Why are Miles and Francesca's problems her problems as well?

Because there is a strong magnetic pull between Miles and Anna, that's why. And, on the night when Anna collapses in hysterical grief in the kitchen, neither of them is able to resist that pull. And the trusting Francesca is in bed upstairs.

It's a mess. Miles loves Francesca – he just loves Anna more. He wants to get out of the marriage without hurting Francesca – but he can't. When Francesca comes clean to Miles about her age he's really stymied. He knows it's obviously a huge issue with her. To call off the wedding because of that would be like dealing a death-blow. He simply can't do it.

Miles can see only one way out – if Anna tells him that his love for her is reciprocated, then he will call off the wedding. Anna is furious. She refuses to say she loves him. If Miles wants to call off the wedding then 'don't make me your excuse'. Then she goes and howls on Milly's shoulder. It's awful.

And so the wedding goes ahead.

Rachel Fielding isn't perfect. She's actually quite sick. For while she has appeared in Nick Hancock's single-dad comedy *Holding the Baby* and played one of Nigel Havers' love interests in *A Perfect Hero*, she has also been wheeled into *Casualty*. Twice.

She's better now.

FRANCESCA TO ANNA ON THE ONE AND ONLY TIME MILES ATTEMPTED TO COOK:
'Typical. They can't just cook, can they? They have to *suffer.*'

FRANCESCA:

'I'm dying to meet this Rachel. Every time I hear about her she's grown another head.'

THIS Quiz

1 What words are on the inside of Anna's kitchen cupboard?
a) Kindly refrain from helping yourself
b) What's mine is yours
c) Anna's cupboard. Fuck off

2 Who is Bridget the Midget?
a) Miles's ex-squeeze
b) Milly's first, disastrous client
c) A naff figurine in Cockroach's café

3 What is Miles's surname?
a) B'stard b) Stewart c) Copeland

4 What is Egg's surname?
a) Cook b) Fry c) Benedict

5 Who is worried about cancer, and why?
a) Anna, for obvious reasons
b) Egg, because of food additives
c) Milly, because she's uptight

6 What's Delilah's boyfriend called?
a) Crackhead b) Blueblood c) Truelove

7 What road is the house in?
a) Benjamin Street b) Sesame Street
c) Peyton Place

8 Who thought calling who a 'total inadequate' was too flattering?
a) Warren: Delilah b) Anna: Miles
c) Miles: his father

9 What's the name of the café where they often have lunch?
a) Central Perk b) Ted's Plaice
c) Conti's Sandwich Shop

10 Who said of the recently decorated house 'This'll be nice when it's finished'?
a) Kira b) Warren's friend Phil
c) Egg's father Jerry

120

11 Who said about what 'I've wanted it as long as I can remember'?
a) Miles: sex
b) Anna: the law
c) Milly: Rachel's sudden and violent death

12 Which twosome always capitulates and does the washing up?
a) Warren and Milly
b) Anna and Miles
c) Ferdy and Egg

13 Under the law, what counts as adultery?
a) A heterosexual act of penetration
b) Any act of penetration
c) Ninety per cent of Anna's sexual exploits

14 Who invited who to 'shake my maracas'?
a) Warren: Ferdy's father
b) Anna: a complete stranger
c) Lenny: Miles

15 Who was abducted by aliens from Planet Poof?
a) Miles b) Ferdy c) Graham

16 Who's breakfast consists of a fag, a vitamin pill and a cup of coffee?
a) Everyone's b) Anna's c) Ferdy's

17 What is a Snag?
a) A sensitive new age guy
b) A bad snog
c) A sexually neurotic ageing gonzo

18 Who bought a posh dress from Harvey Nichols?
a) Mill, b) Anna c) Patsy

19 Why did Pemberton get into bed with Locke?
a) Why the hell do you think?
b) Because he was cold
c) Because they are business partners

20 Who wears nasty Y-fronts?
a) Jerry b) O'Donnell c) Milly

21 Who fancies Anthea Turner?
a) Hooperman b) Egg c) Jo

22 Who didn't have telephone sex?
a) Egg and Milly, b) Ferdy and Lenny
c) Miles and Delilah

23 What team does Nicky support?
a) Leyton Orient b) Man United c) Arsenal

24 Who had a raunchy dream about Michael Portillo?
a) Anna b) Ferdy c) Peter Lilley

25 What did the house buy for Warren's leaving present?
a) Pink sequinned Judy Garland rollerblades
b) A Versace jacket
c) A blow-up policeman

26 Who did Anna snog in a nightclub?
a) Warren b) Sarah Newley
c) She can't remember

27 Who bought Colombian crap?
a) Ferdy b) Miles c) Egg

28 Who chundered in a taxi?
a) Miles b) Anna c) Kira

29 Who said 'I just want to have a long bath'?
a) Milly b) Milly c) Milly

30 Whose wall socket was loose?
a) Ferdy's b) Anna's c) O'Donnell's

31 Who failed to pick up who at Euston Station?
a) Milly: Nat b) Ferdy: anyone
c) Miles: Francesca

32 Who threatened to scalp Kelly's trolls?
a) Kira b) Jo c) O'Donnell

33 Who helped themselves to Anna's Clinique?

a) Miles b) Francesca c) Ferdy

34 Who has been lying about her age?

a) Barbara Cartland

b) Kelly

c) Francesca

35 Who thought Miles might have 'a wonger the size of my arm'?

a) Lenny b) Hooperman c) Kira

36 Who buys dresses, wears them for a night and then takes them back to the shop?

a) Anna b) Kelly c) Warren

37 What wedding present did the house buy for Miles?

a) A book on older women

b) Cosmetic surgery vouchers

c) A large furry dog on wheels

38 Who didn't have sex in a loo?

a) Milly and Egg

b) Ferdy and Lenny

c) Warren and practically everyone

'I love you Anna.
I always have and I always will.'

Now that *is* touching. Sweet and spoken from the heart.
The only problem is that the lovestruck Miles is about to marry Francesca, not Anna.

We knew trouble was brewing when Anna accompanied the boys on the stag night. A less likely honorary bloke you could scarcely imagine – all white lycra halterneck and black stilettos – but Anna acquitted herself with aplomb and set the tone for the evening by downing her first pint in one.

Miles was in his element, even if none of his other friends were able to come. We didn't care – we've never met them (do they exist?) and didn't want strangers cluttering up what looked to be a pretty promising evening. Miles was with his best mates: Anna, Egg and Jo. Even Ferdy was there ('I s'ppose he's a kind of bloke'), demonstrating that he does actually possess clothes apart from his biking leathers.

The only one missing from the happy family was Milly. But Milly had just discovered that O'Donnell was still playing happy families with his own wife, so she ignored Egg's message and went to bed with a bottle of vodka and large measures of grief, horror and guilt.

Miles, for his part, wanted to turn the stag night into a shag night and to go to bed with Anna. The evening had made him maudlin and when they returned to the house he declared himself to her. It wasn't just the booze talking; he really did want to call off the wedding. But we know what Anna said to that. Before going to bed and crying herself to sleep.

All in all, the stag night was a rousing, tone-setting build-up to...

THAT Wedding

Miles tells Jo that, yes, he can invite Kira to the reception:
'Go ahead, it's your funeral.'
JO: **'Yours, you mean, you mad bastard.'**

What They Wore:

The bride wore white

A small part of Anna was covered in a lilac mini-dress

Milly wore a long lime-green number with black boxing gloves

Kira agonised for ages about 'something really smart' and turned up in a denim jacket (but with a Little Black Dress underneath)

Rachel had her hair stapled to her head

Miles wore a collarless jacket (it looked suspiciously like the Paul Smith number that Egg dismissed as 'very eighties')

Lenny twirled in a kilt

Ferdy lifted Lenny's kilt

What They Said:

Miles and Francesca said **'I do'**

Anna said **'I am not going to cry'**

Rachel said **'I suppose you'll be needing someone else now? For the house, I mean.'**

Milly said **'There's something about you I really can't stand'**

Rachel said **'Working late together, meetings... you feel like you're intruding half the time.'**

Egg said **'She's been sleeping with O'Donnell, hasn't she?'**

Egg said **'I've realised now why people cry at weddings'**

Francesca said **'Weird speech. What was all that about?'**

Milly said **'It was Rachel, wasn't it? She told him.'**

Ferdy said **'I love you.'**

Rachel said **'It wasn't me!'**

John Paul Young sang **'Love is in the Air'** as Milly barrelled up to Rachel and thumped her

Warren said **'Outstanding!'**

Nearly five million people said **'We want another series.'**

THIS PRESS LIFE

'The programme that made BBC 2 cool again.' **DAILY EXPRESS**

'Its writers and directors have tackled television's greatest taboos and come up with a winning formula.' **THE TIMES**

'I did not regularly watch *This Life*, but caught the final episode and was appalled at the drugs, booze and, worst of all, simulated sex between homosexuals... We should complain more often and perhaps our comments would have some weight in preventing such trash being shown.' **DAILY MAIL**

'If you've never seen it you might be confusing it with *That's Life*, which was something very different, featuring as it did a mad woman in low-cut chiffon going on about amusing menu misprints and suggestive-looking parsnips.' **THE INDEPENDENT**

'*This Life* is about *this* life; this one here.' **THE GUARDIAN**

'I am obsessed with *This Life*. So is everyone else.' **EVENING STANDARD**

'The destruction of young minds proceeds apace and a demoralised public has stopped even protesting about it.' **YORKSHIRE POST**

'Britain's best crinoline-free TV series.' **THE OBSERVER**

'The Independent Television Commission is considering banning smoking on television when it appears to glamorize the habit.' **THE TIMES**

'*This Life* is now said to dominate conversation at every smart dinner-party in London.' **EVENING STANDARD**

'It's talked about at all the right dinner-parties.' **DAILY EXPRESS**

'Is it a posh soap with plenty of how's your father thrown in?' **THE GUARDIAN**

'The dreaded yuppie has returned, rising from its unsealed designer tomb to haunt us once more... Jenkins has created some of the most immediately detestable stereotypes possible.' **THE SCOTSMAN**

'Loathed by the Establishment, adored by the eternally youthful.' **DAILY EXPRESS**

'This is Brown-Blair's Britain. Joy tends to be fleeting, and introduced by chemicals or the prospect of Anna.' **THE GUARDIAN**

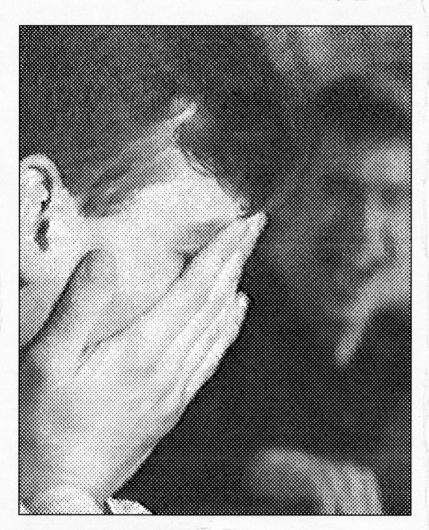

THIS PINCH OF SALT...

'The final cliff-hanging episode of the cult TV drama *This Life* was seen by more than 5 million people.'
THE GUARDIAN

'BBC 2's cult drama *This Life* ended its run with an impressive 3.5 million viewers'
BROADCAST

'The nation's 4.23 million *This Life* junkies tuned in to savour their final fix.'
INDEPENDENT ON SUNDAY

The official viewing figures were 4.2 million for the last episode with 1.4 million watching the repeat.

THIS POST-SCRIPT...

'The BBC's controversial series *This Life* has signed off with an official inquiry into its bad language and graphic sex... the outrage centred on a gay sex scene in a lavatory. One of the lead characters and his Scottish boyfriend were seen in what a BBC spokesman described as "post coital delight".
The two had earlier been seen taking drugs.'
DAILY MAIL

'Broadcasters have been accused of feeling free to push back the boundaries of taste and decency because the Government – including openly homosexual Cultural Secretary Chris Smith – is seen as soft on censorship.' **GUESS WHICH PAPER?**

'While some viewers will doubtless whip up the familiar storm about the language, nudity and explicit sex, others will welcome a drama which, without being coy or aggressive, shows young people behaving as they actually do behave...'
FINANCIAL TIMES

'Roll over Rumpole, and tell Kavanagh QC the news – young lawyers today, like most people their age, are sorted for Es and whizz.'
THE STAGE

'It will be sorely missed.'
THE INDEPENDENT

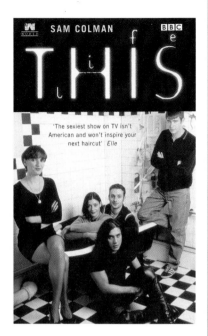

'The sexiest show on TV isn't American and won't inspire your next haircut' *Elle*

Other *THIS Life* titles available

BBC / PENGUIN BOOKS

THIS Life by Sam Colman

Now the series of the decade is a novel. Follow the lives and loves of the house-sharing twenty-something lawyers from the first two series, as they stumble through nineties London amid overflowing ashtrays and hangovers from hell in this official tie-in book.

ISBN 0 14 027431 6

BBC VIDEO

Three BBC videos featuring the first series of *THIS Life*, including:

Coming Together; Happy Families; Living Dangerously; Sex, Lies and Muesli Yoghurt

Fantasy Football; Family Outing; Brief Encounter; Cheap Thrills

Just Sex; Father Figure; Let's Get It On

Running times: 147 minutes, 154 minutes, 113 minutes approx.
BBCV 6470, BBCV 6471, BBCV 6472

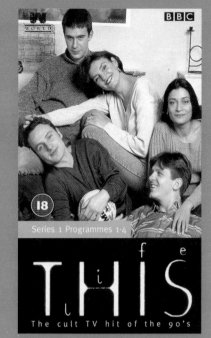

Series 1 Programmes 1-4

The cult TV hit of the 90's

Series 1 Programmes 5-8

The cult TV hit of the 90's

Series 1 Programmes 9-11

The cult TV hit of the 90's